## "Okay, Fantasy, what would Babycakes do now?" Brigitte asked teasingly

"She'd..." Charlie swallowed hard. "She'd be trying to distract Fantasy Fuzz."

Something in Brigitte snapped. *Distract him? He wanted to be distracted? She'd show him distraction!* "You mean like this?" she purred, putting her hands on his shoulders and leaning close enough for her thigh to graze his.

*Go ahead, devour me,* her eyes challenged. "Your move now, Fantasy."

*His move?* Charlie was immobilized by his powerful desire for her. But Brigitte was only performing the role he'd assigned her.

How would Fantasy deal with Brigitte's overture? He imagined a cartoon panel of Fantasy Fuzz with Babycakes Brigitte writhing in his arms. The thought drove him over the edge. Leaning over her, he gave her a kiss to end all kisses....

Readers of **Glenda Sanders**'s *Island Nights* loved Brigitte, the spirited, vivacious younger sister of hero Stephen Dumont, and begged Glenda to give her a book of her own. When Glenda enthusiastically started considering the idea, it seemed obvious to her that she needed a hero at the other end of the spectrum from Brigitte—virile yet reserved, even bashful. She came up with Charlie Battle, a cartoonist with a chauvinist detective character named Fantasy Fuzz who calls vampy women "Babycakes." How to throw them together? What better event than a murder-mystery weekend at which Brigitte and Charlie could test each other in the sexy, suspenseful roles of Babycakes and Fantasy Fuzz.

## Books by Glenda Sanders

HARLEQUIN TEMPTATION
300–ISLAND NIGHTS
316–DARK SECRETS
356–A HUMAN TOUCH

# Babycakes

## GLENDA SANDERS

# *Harlequin Books*

TORONTO • NEW YORK • LONDON
AMSTERDAM • PARIS • SYDNEY • HAMBURG
STOCKHOLM • ATHENS • TOKYO • MILAN
MADRID • WARSAW • BUDAPEST • AUCKLAND

Published February 1992

ISBN 0-373-25483-0

BABYCAKES

# 1

"RUNNING LATE?"

Brigitte Dumont scowled at her brother Stephen's question as she settled opposite him with her salad plate. It was obvious from the fact that the dining room was almost deserted and Stephen was the only other Dumont left in the place, that she was *very* late for lunch.

"Never a dull moment in Special Events!" she replied. "Donna Prescott called as I was walking out of my office. She's sold *Contemporary Canada* on the idea of an advance feature on the mystery weekend."

"*Contemporary Canada*. That's quite a coup."

"Let's just hope the event's a sellout," Brigitte said, plunging a fork into her spinach salad. "BARF needs the money."

BARF—the Banff Area Recycling Foundation—was on the verge of securing a principle investor for a recycling center in the Bow Valley. The murder-mystery weekend scheduled at the Chalet Dumont was to be a fund-raiser for BARF's campaign to create local public awareness of the need for the center.

"After they got C. H. Battle, BARF had a guaranteed sellout," Stephen remarked.

"He certainly piqued Donna's interest. She was teaming with questions about him. She's coming over to interview him tonight."

"Who wouldn't be curious about the creator of the world's hottest new comic strip?"

"Frankly, I don't understand what all the excitement is about," Brigitte said. "*Fantasy Fuzz* is a sexist joke. There's a buxom woman in every story line, and Fantasy Fuzz calls every one of them 'Babycakes.'"

"That's what makes him fun—he's so outrageous, he's camp."

"I don't see the appeal myself. But if C.H. Battle is willing to write a murder-mystery scenario featuring the Dumonts and is willing to play Fantasy Fuzz all weekend for BARF out of the goodness of his heart, and if his presence is getting a preview article in *Contemporary Canada*, then he has my gratitude."

"I understand he's single," Stephen said. "Given your current situation, perhaps you should—"

"What situation?"

"You were the chief topic of conversation at lunch."

Brigitte groaned. "What have I done now?"

"Jennifer took great pleasure in announcing that her Aunt Brigitte has to get married." Brigitte groaned again. Jennifer was almost twelve—an age when young girls are given to drama and making cataclysmic statements.

"That must have created a mild sensation."

"There was some wild speculation for a few minutes. I told everyone it must be that banker from Switzerland. You should have played a little harder to get, eh?"

Brigitte gave her brother an exasperated look. She had fought off the ardent advances of that slimy Swiss banker for two full weeks—under the amused scrutiny of her family.

"But Jennifer said no, it wasn't the banker at all. She said it was because Nicole wants a French bra."

"That must have made her mother's day."

"There were a number of hysterical *mon Dieu*'s. Then our dear mother reminded Claire that when *she* was thirteen, the issue was black lace panties, and Claude created a little excitement by announcing that Claire *still* wears black lace panties. That's when Claire really lost it and threatened to sue for divorce if he said one more word in front of the girls."

"A typical Dumont family lunch." Brigitte grinned. "Naturally, *I* miss all the fun."

"Umm," Stephen agreed, as the waiter refilled his coffee cup. When the waiter moved out of earshot, he said, "Everyone seemed to understand but me—what does Nicole's wanting a French bra have to do with your getting married?"

Brigitte sighed. "It was the last straw. The *coup de maître*. Yesterday I found a gray hair!"

"I don't see what either has to do with getting married."

"A man wouldn't," Brigitte said wryly. "*Your* biological clock's not ticking away into oblivion."

"My clock has ticked years longer than yours, baby sister."

"Yes, but your wife—who happens to be younger than I am—is glowingly pregnant. And my niece, the one I used to rock to sleep, wants a French bra." She hesitated, then added, "This morning I overheard a college boy refer to me as an older woman."

"He must have noticed the gray hair."

Brigitte ignored the gibe. "I'm going to be twenty-nine on my next birthday, and after that I'll be thirty." She paused long enough to fix Stephen with a slightly accusatory glare. "It's not exactly easy watching your wife waddling around here blissfully pregnant, knowing that she's younger than I am. No offense."

"None taken. But, Brigitte, you can't just get married because you find a gray hair. You have to find the right person."

"I'll just have to start looking, then."

"You've been looking ever since you got your first bottle of perfume," Stephen said. "Père commented on that at lunch."

"I suppose my penchant for perfume came into the conversation shortly after Claire's underwear."

"Immediately following the divorce threats," Stephen confirmed.

Brigitte ate her salad in silence, then thinking out loud said, "If I put my mind to it, I ought to be able to find someone nice to settle down with. Men seem to find me appealing."

"According to your elder niece, you're surrounded by men who find you irresistibly sexy. She thinks perhaps if she had a French bra, she could give you some competition."

Brigitte nodded. "She may be right. She's already drawing some interested looks. I'd better grab an eligible man while I still have a good selection, eh? Once she gets that French bra, I'll have stiff competition."

"You have at least two years before you have to worry about that, if Claire has anything to say about it," Stephen assured her.

Brigitte glanced at her watch. "Unfortunately I don't have two years before our special guest arrives. He said any time after two. I'd better get going in case he's early."

"This Battle guy's bound to be making millions on *Fantasy Fuzz*," Stephen pointed out. "Maybe you can bag him."

"I don't think I could ever be serious about a man who makes his living drawing a cartoon detective who calls women Babycakes."

"He's environmentally conscious."

"Yes. And for that I'll be gracious to him. That doesn't mean I have to marry him." She grinned at her brother and teased, "Besides, if I get too desperate, I can break a leg and you can ship me off to an island to be rescued by a handsome prince, eh?"

"The odds of that happening twice in the same family are remote," Stephen replied. He had met his wife, Janet, on Barbados while recuperating from a broken leg. "You'll just have to find your own route to romantic magic."

"Romantic magic," Brigitte repeated thoughtfully. She'd always enjoyed the company of the opposite sex. Yet lately, the courtship game, with all its flirting and cat-and-mouse, had seemed empty—much like her bed at night. While the Chalet Dumont provided her with an endless supply of men with whom to play the game, precious few had made it past the doors of her private quarters. Maybe a little romantic magic *was* what she needed.

"I'll keep that suggestion in mind," she said, rising to leave. "But right now—"

She made a quick trip to her suite to freshen up before heading for her office to await C. H. Battle's arrival. No matter what she thought of Fantasy Fuzz's attitude toward women, Battle was an important guest, and she wanted to be in top form when she met him. After putting on fresh lip gloss, she drove a brush through her ponytail, then fluffed it.

"Adorable, as usual," she told her reflection in the mirror, then chuckled as she tossed the hairbrush in her vanity. Yes, C. H. Battle was going to get the full treatment. *She* might think *Fantasy Fuzz* was a sexist crock, but the rest of the world adored him; and because they adored him, they would pay well to spend a weekend with Fantasy's creator as he ran around in a Fantasy Fuzz bombardier jacket, pretending to solve a homicide.

Apparently, no one in BARF had expected Battle to agree to play Fuzz. On a long shot, they'd extended the invitation because Battle had been one of the charter members of BARF long before *Fantasy Fuzz* became a hit comic strip.

Not that he'd been an active member. Brigitte had learned that no one had even connected the "Charles Battle" on BARF's membership roster with the famous cartoonist until Marjorie Ambrose, who was in charge of the annual Environmental Awareness poster-design contest, happened across an old poster bearing Battle's distinctive signature. After discovering that the Charles Battle on their list was indeed the C. H. Battle who drew *Fantasy Fuzz*, Marjorie had then arranged with Brigitte that the original three-year-old poster would be auctioned off during the mystery weekend, along with a Fantasy Fuzz leather jacket and other signature merchandise donated by the syndicate distributing the comic strip.

Brigitte detoured through the kitchen on her way to the lobby and her office. Monday nights—Family Night at the Chalet Dumont—were busy even during off-season, so the kitchen was abuzz with preparations for the dinner crowd. Brigitte wove through the maze of workstations to the dessert-making area, where she found the pastry chef supervising the assembly of a multitiered cake.

Spying Brigitte, the chef nodded. Stepping back from the chaos, he waved his hand in the air dramatically. "Another cake, another artistic achievement."

Brigitte returned his warm smile. "Yes, another masterpiece."

*"Mais oui,"* Gérard teased, exaggerating his accent. "I am an *artiste, n'est pas?"*

Brigitte cleared her throat in mock authority. "I was just making sure you weren't doing anything too artsy—like having a woman burst out of it wearing a sash that says Babycakes."

Gérard slapped his forehead. *"Mon Dieu,* why didn't I think of that in time to hire a model?"

"Because you like working at the Chalet Dumont," Brigitte suggested wryly.

Gérard grinned affably and shrugged. He was a cherub of a man with a disposition as sweet as the confections he created, and he was in about as much danger of being fired as Brigitte was of being disinherited, and he knew it. "The cake will be beautiful, and tastefully done," he assured her. "All of the Bow Valley will be talking about it tomorrow."

"Let's hope so," Brigitte said. "The whole point of having a Fantasy Fuzz cake tonight is to get people talking about the murder-mystery weekend."

"Brigitte?"

She cocked an eyebrow.

"Do you think you might...that you could ask...I saved last Sunday's comics. If C. H. Battle would just sign it—"

"Drop your paper off at the desk and I'll see what I can do."

"Oh, *merci!*"

"Do you like the *Fantasy Fuzz* strip that much?" Brigitte asked, surprised by his tongue-tied enthusiasm.

"Oh, *oui*. This C. H. Battle is very clever. I'm never sure who did it until the final installment. But this time...this time, I'm sure it's the woman, the victim's sister-in-law, the one Fantasy calls—"

"Babycakes?" Brigitte supplied.

"*Oui. Babycakes.* I am using that concept on the cake, putting petits fours on the ledge of one tier. Do you get it? Petits fours—little cakes. Baby cakes."

"Now *that's* clever," Brigitte said. *More clever than making a fortune drawing voluptuous women who allow themselves to be called Babycakes and moan, "Oh, Fantasy!" when kissed.*

"I'm piping little women on the petits fours."

"Little women?"

"Tiny icing women." Gérard gestured with his thumb and forefinger to indicate how tiny the icing figurines would be. "Blondes, brunettes, redheads."

Brigitte rolled her eyes. *Icing women on baby cakes!* The whole world was going Fantasy Fuzz crazy!

CHARLIE BATTLE still felt self-conscious walking into places like the Chalet Dumont. His plunge into fame and fortune was so recent that he had yet to feel as if he belonged in a resort frequented by the affluent.

He'd seen the chalet many times, of course. Almost anyone who spent time on the lake or the slopes was familiar with the picturesque Chalet Dumont, with its overhanging roofs that made it look as if it might have been transported into the Canadian Rockies from a mountainside in the Swiss Alps. Over the years it had become a Banff institution noted for both its elegance and its sense of fun.

Charlie wasn't sure what he'd been expecting when he walked inside—the stiff formality of a big-city deluxe hotel, perhaps—but the informality of the high-ceilinged lobby was a welcome surprise. The focal point of the room was a circular fire pit that, in winter, would provide a welcome oasis of heat for chilled skiers coming in from the slopes. Now, pots of ivy and red and white geraniums were a cheery, warm-weather substitute for a roaring fire. The sight of that bright patchwork of red and white and the frivolous meanderings of the ivy boughs somehow made Charlie feel more comfortable with his decision to participate in the murder-mystery weekend for BARF.

He'd planned on declining the request until he'd mentioned it to Joe Blanning, publicist for the syndicate distributing the *Fantasy Fuzz* comic strip. Joe had gone wild over the prospect of positive publicity. "Some press featuring C. H. Battle as a concerned environmentalist will help take the edge off *Fantasy Fuzz's* hard-core image," he'd said. "I'll see if I can't generate some wide coverage."

So Charlie had agreed to write a mystery scenario featuring the Dumont family and to dress up like Fantasy Fuzz to hunt down the murderer at a BARF benefit weekend.

This preparatory visit was also a chance to finally meet the Dumonts—whom he had been curious about since he'd first come to Banff—including the famous patriarch, Jean-Pierre Dumont, a skier who'd turned Olympic gold into a gold mine. Charlie had heard that old Jean-Pierre had been quite a rounder in his bachelor days.

At the age of forty, Jean Pierre had fallen madly in love with the young and beautiful Marguerite, married her and become an exemplary family man. Then he had busied himself transforming what had been a mediocre ski chalet into a Banff institution.

The hotel clerk snapped to attention when Charlie stepped up to the registration desk. "May I help you, sir?"

"I'm supposed to have a room reserved. C. H. Battle."

"Oh, yes, sir," the clerk replied, flicking a card from an alphabetized file and skimming it briefly before sliding it across the counter. "If you'll just fill this out, Brigitte will show you to your suite."

"I can manage on my own if you'll just give me directions."

The young man colored slightly, flustered. "But—"

"I've only got the one bag, and I'm perfectly capable of carrying it myself."

"We never argue with our guests," said a melodious voice from behind him. A decidedly *female* voice, with just the proper blend of softness and sultriness to rouse his libido. He turned and found the source of the voice smiling up at him, all bright blue eyes, glossy red lips and rich, dark, bouncing ponytail.

"I'm Brigitte Dumont," she said, holding out her hand. "Welcome to the chalet, Mr. Battle."

Charlie inhaled a whiff of perfume as his hand enveloped hers. Ordinarily he found perfume cloying, and usually it made him sneeze, but this...this was rather like fresh air high on a mountainside—crisp and clear, but unmistakably feminine. It produced a physical response in him that was far removed from a nose-tickling urge to sneeze. He managed an appropriate comment about being glad to be there, but found himself wondering if her lips were naturally glossy or if she put something on them to make them shine.

Brigitte extracted her hand from his to accept the key the desk clerk had lifted from a row of hooks on the wall behind him, then looked up at Charlie again. Her smile was slightly crooked. For a second, Charlie fantasized about tracing her lips with his fingertips.

"You're more than welcome to carry your own bags," Brigitte told him. "But as a special Dumont guest, you're stuck with a Dumont escort."

*Special guest.* He almost told her he was just "good old Charlie" and she needn't bother. The power of celebrity still sometimes niggled like an ill-fitting shoe, reminding him of the before-and-after quality of his life. At times he felt like screaming that he was the same person now that he had been all those years he'd spent doodling one cartoon strip after another, hoping for one to be picked up by a syndicate.

"Just follow me," Brigitte said exuberantly. "I promise to make it as painless as possible."

Charlie picked up his suitcase. "Lead the way, Babycakes."

Brigitte fumed silently as they waited for the elevator. *Babycakes!* Who did this Battle guy think he was—Fantasy Fuzz?

"Did you have a pleasant trip?" she asked, as the elevator ascended.

"Uneventful." An hour's drive on roads he'd traveled dozens of times could hardly be classified as thrilling.

*So much for conversation,* Brigitte thought. Obviously Mr. C. H. Battle was the strong, silent type—as well as the rugged and virile type. Who would have expected a man who drew cartoons for a living to be so broad chested?

Sensing his perusal of her, she gave him a sidelong glance, then made a lame attempt at a casual smile when her gaze met his and discovered pure male heat. The air in the elevator car suddenly seemed close and still. When the doors opened at the third-floor landing, she gratefully stepped out into the hallway. Walking briskly toward the minisuite reserved for him, Brigitte was intensely aware of Mr. C. H. Battle's presence behind her.

The majesty of the Rocky Mountains greeted them through two scenic windows. Brigitte unfolded the luggage rack for his suitcase and dangled the room key in front of Battle's nose. "Your key, sir. I trust you'll find the accommodations satisfactory. If not, just dial 0 for the desk and ask for one of the Dumonts and we'll take care of you."

*Don't I wish!* Charlie thought, still fixated on her lips. He reached for the key but instead of taking it, wrapped his fingers around her hand, trapping the key between their palms. The cool metal quickly warmed as he peered down at her face. "Am I allowed to request a particular Dumont?"

Brigitte delicately drew her hand away, but didn't break the intimate eye contact he'd established. "We Dumonts are pretty interchangeable."

His gaze held the same smoldering intensity as it had in the elevator. "I doubt that."

She lifted her eyebrows jauntily. "Then specify."

"I will," he promised.

A knock at the door caught them both by surprise. Brigitte gestured, inviting him to answer it.

The uniformed bellboy held a large gift basket wrapped in cellophane and tied with a ribbon. "Mr. C. H. Battle?"

"Himself," Charlie replied.

The young man thrust the basket toward Charlie. "Compliments of the management."

Charlie gave Brigitte a sardonic grin over the handle of the basket. "You shouldn't have."

He put the basket down, then reached into his pocket, but when he opened his wallet, the bellboy said, "Oh, no, sir. That's not necessary." The boy glanced at Brigitte, and then back at Charlie. "It's compliments of the management."

"I insist," Charlie continued. "And I have it on good authority that the staff of the Chalet Dumont does not argue with its guests." He shot Brigitte a triumphant look as he pressed a folded bill into the young man's hand.

"Thank you, sir," the young man responded, then hesitantly added, in rapid-fire speech, "Mr. Battle, I read *Fantasy Fuzz* every day. He's awesome, the way he solves cases and—every police department should have a detective like Fuzz, eh?"

"Too bad he's only a comic-strip character," Brigitte said. "We could eliminate crime entirely if he were real."

The bellboy extracted a folded strip of newspaper from his breast pocket. "I clipped this from today's paper. If you wouldn't mind—"

"Of course," Charlie said. He carried the comic strip to the desk and autographed it, then returned it to the young man, who thanked him warmly before leaving.

Charlie turned his attention to the gift basket, poking and probing through the cellophane. "What have we here?"

"Just a little something to make your visit with us a little more pleasurable."

"Fruit, cheese—*wine?*" Lifting the bottle from the basket, he studied the label. "No Dom Pérignon champagne? I'm disappointed."

"You're the first man I've ever known to actually admit to *liking* champagne," Brigitte responded. "We assume that our male guests would prefer a dry Moselle. I'd be happy to call room service and exchange it."

Slightly embarrassed, Charlie confessed. "I was only teasing about the Dom Pérignon."

"So was I," Brigitte replied with an impish smile. "We don't stock it, except at New Year's."

Charlie snuffled in surprise. "You were bluffing?"

"Gotcha!" Brigitte said, mischief dancing in her eyes.

Charlie had an uneasy feeling that he could easily be "gotten" by her on more than a bluff about champagne. He reminded himself that she was there to pamper C. H. Battle and not because she'd chosen to be in the company of plain ole Charlie. Why not just enjoy the fact that Brigitte was there, smelling sweeter than spring mountain air and smiling brightly at him, he told himself. Suddenly he had the urge to know everything about her.

"Family Night kicks off at seven, but you're invited to my parents' suite at six to meet the family. We've got a feature writer for *Contemporary Canada* coming, too."

Charlie nodded to indicate he was listening, but his mind was not on the impending evening with the Dumont family. He was focused—body, mind and senses— on the woman standing barely an arm's length away. She was close enough that if he extended his arm, he'd be able to touch her. But she was leaving. The invitation to her parents' suite was a wrap-up, a departure speech delivered as effortlessly as her welcoming repartee.

It was obvious that dispensing hospitality came easily to her. She was a Dumont, after all, and bred to it. He envied her comfortable confidence—that type of confidence which grew out of knowing exactly who you were and where you belonged.

She had moved to the door. Her fingers were wrapped around the knob. "You probably want to get settled in after your drive. Remember, if you need anything—"

A simple twist of her wrist, and the door was open. She was about to walk through it and close it behind her. Charlie realized suddenly how very much he didn't want her to leave—and that he hadn't the foggiest idea how to ask her to stay.

Charlie had spent most of his life in awe of the female species—baffled by their effect on him, yearning to relate to them, envious of men who were at ease with them. In his twenties he'd managed to master some of his debilitating shyness, but women remained a mystery to him. Here he was, C. H. Battle, world-famous cartoonist, with a delectable woman just brimming over with the need to be accommodating, and he didn't even know how to coax her into sticking around for a while.

*Fuzz wouldn't let her just walk out. Think, Battle. How would Fuzz handle this situation?*

"Hey, Babycakes."

Brigitte paused in the doorway and looked back at him. "Were you talking to me?"

Charlie picked up the bottle of wine by the neck and held it up. "Does the Dumont hospitality stretch to include keeping a lonely man company?"

Her eyes narrowed and Charlie experienced a small thrill that the suggestion had given her pause. He wasn't accustomed to making women nervous.

"I hate drinking alone," he pressed. It sounded corny, even to him. He didn't care. He simply hoped it worked.

Brigitte hesitated before shaking her head slowly in exasperation, letting him know she knew she was being manipulated. Then, shrugging her shoulders, she smiled that crooked smile again, stepped back inside the room and closed the door behind her. "We can't have one of our honored guests drinking alone in the middle of the afternoon, eh?"

She walked to the small bar area of the suite and picked up the plastic ice bucket. "I'll get some ice to chill it. The machine's just down the hall."

He watched her cross the room again, captivated by the graceful but energetic way she moved. Her skirt swayed, producing a whisper of sound, while her ponytail swished in defiance of the ribbon that anchored it. It seemed to him that her presence lingered in the room after she was gone. The image of her face clung in his mind as he stared idly out the huge window.

An undercurrent of excitement flowed through his veins, a sensation of being on the brink of something new, something unknown and possibly dangerous. And the "something new" he was on the brink of . . . was Brigitte Dumont.

# 2

BRIGITTE HAD LEFT the door to Charlie's suite ajar and it slid open noiselessly when she returned from the ice machine. Charlie stood near the window, apparently absorbed in the sight of the mountains, and Brigitte took advantage of his preoccupation to study him. With his hands hooked in the hip pockets of his pants in the stance of a little boy staring at the horizon and daydreaming, he hardly looked the world-famous celebrity she'd expected.

Brigitte was just about to jiggle the ice pail to make her presence known when he seemed to sense that she was there and turned to face her. He took his hands from his pockets and squared his shoulders. "Nice view."

"The best in Banff," Brigitte agreed, sliding the ice bucket onto the table.

*But not as intriguing as your face,* Charlie thought. *Not as bedeviling as the perfume you wear.* He'd smelled her fragrance rather than heard her enter the room. "You've lived here at the chalet all your life?"

"Uh-hmm," Brigitte replied.

"It must be nice to grow up in a place with a view from every window." *Is that why you glow?*

Brigitte eased the wine bottle into the ice and smiled. "When I was a little girl, I didn't realize there were windows without mountains outside."

"I didn't see a mountain until I was fourteen." Before that, the center of his life had been a modest house in Chicago. He always remembered that house with longing for the contentment he'd known there—a contentment based on his childhood belief that nothing bad would ever happen.

"You're not a native of the area, then?"

"My mother is." An expression of pain passed fleetingly over his face. "We moved here after my father died."

"You were only fourteen?"

He nodded.

Brigitte thought of her niece, Nicole, and how vulnerable she was at almost fourteen. "That must have been awful for you."

Charlie shrugged away the sympathy. "I survived it." But it had robbed him of his youth and his faith in his own invulnerability.

In the silence that followed, Brigitte spun the neck of the wine bottle expertly between her palms. Charlie noticed her slim wrists, the delicate taper of her fingers, the sheen of the coral polish on her nails. "You look like you've had a little practice at that."

Relieved to have avoided the subject of death, Brigitte smiled. "Just one of many things you pick up growing up in a chalet with a public dining room. I had a crush on one of our wine stewards once and followed him around like a lovesick puppy."

"Unrequited love, I take it?" Charlie suggested, although he couldn't imagine a man capable of drawing breath not falling under her charm.

"He was older, he was beautiful—and he was gay," Brigitte explained. "He left at the end of the summer with a bartender from a club in the township. I cried for a day and a half when I found out."

"A day and a half?" Charlie echoed, cocking his eyebrow mockingly.

Brigitte giggled softly; the sound affected him in unexpected ways.

"There was an early snowfall that year," she said. "There were . . . diversions."

"Heterosexual, no doubt," Charlie added, his mind forming images of robust skiers standing in line four-deep at the registration desk, oggling the slopes of Brigitte's body while they waited to check in.

Looking into the deceptive innocence of Brigitte's answering smile and those big, bright, guileless eyes, Charlie resented those skiers who could afford to check into the Chalet Dumont and flirt with Brigitte Dumont instead of taking the ski packages at the modestly-priced hotels in the outlying regions—those young men of wealth and privilege or spoiled Yuppie junior executives on the rise, all of them randy as buck elks during rutting season and equipped with the social aplomb that made them feel entitled to the company of the Brigitte Dumonts of this world. What did any of *them* contribute to society compared to people like his parents, who had eked out a living teaching school or fighting crime?

His resentment seeped over to include Brigitte. Brigitte of the big eyes and shiny lips. What did the Brigitte Dumonts of this world do for society, for that matter—smiling up at the privileged elite and chilling wine for celebrity guests?

*Celebrity guests.* Some ridiculous scribbles on paper had elevated him from the ranks of the anonymous toilers to the status of celebrity deserving of wine and the company of Miss Brigitte Dumont.

*What kind of sense did that make?*

He resented the fact that his success with *Fantasy Fuzz* had put him here at this table across from Brigitte Dumont; but what he resented the most was that he wanted to touch her so badly.

*And why shouldn't he reach for what he wanted, for what his success had earned him?* He'd worked for that success, waited for it, believed it would come to him if he just kept drawing characters original enough and arresting enough to capture the public's imagination. He hadn't asked for Brigitte Dumont. But there she was, across the table from him, chilling wine and smiling at him—the answer to all the frustrated yearnings and unfulfilled desires he'd built up during the lean years of anonymity.

"The glasses," Brigitte said. She left the wine in ice while she walked over to the hospitality tray and tried to concentrate on removing the plastic wrap from the glasses.

Her fingers were trembling—a fact she hid from Charlie by turning her back to him as she worked. Men often looked at her as though she were the main course on a menu. Occasionally she found it insulting, but usually, merely annoying or mildly amusing. Never before had she found herself entertaining thoughts of what it would be like to be devoured.

His effect on her was unnerving, to say the least. She wasn't sure which she wanted or needed most: to grab him by the lapels and pull him close enough to kiss, or a long, cold shower. She suspected the first would be more interesting; the second, more prudent. He was, after all, a special guest of the chalet, and their relationship should be strictly business because of their involvement with BARF.

Unfortunately a cold shower was out of the question at the moment, so she sucked in a deep breath, and carried the glasses to the table . . . and hoped she had the wherewithal not to jump the bones of a man she hardly knew and wasn't even sure she liked.

She gave the wine a final swirl in the icy water, then lifted it from the bucket, blotted it with a hand towel and presented it to him. "You can do the macho stuff. There's a fold-out corkscrew in the basket."

"So that's what that funny-looking thing was," Charlie said, rummaging for it among the packets of gourmet cheese.

"We'd never have attracted the attention of *Contemporary Canada* if you hadn't agreed to script the mystery for BARF," Brigitte told him, resisting the urge to show Charlie how to unfold the corkscrew.

"I'm glad old Fuzz is good for something," Charlie responded. He'd mastered the assembly and was twisting the metal worm into the cork with masculine concentration.

"The reporter is a friend of mine. She does good work." Brigitte watched Charlie's hand maneuver the corkscrew with a blend of finesse and strength, and tried not to let her imagination run amok considering other things those hands might be good at.

The bottle surrendered the cork with a loud gasp, and Brigitte and Charlie exchanged surprised grins. "Who needs champagne?" Brigitte said, with laughter in her voice.

"Certainly not us," Charlie agreed. But as he poured the wine, he wished it was champagne. He wished the squatty hotel glasses were champagne flutes. He wished—for the first time in his life—that he was wearing a tuxedo, and Brigitte, something slinky and sexy. And most of all, he wished that she was with him because she wanted to be with him and not because she was the innkeeper's daughter and he, the "celebrity" guest.

"To a successful murder-mystery weekend and BARF," Brigitte declared, raising her glass.

"Hear, hear." Charlie clinked his glass against hers gently. *A toast. Of course. How socially correct. How gracious. How appropriate.* He wondered if Brigitte Dumont had, in her entire life, ever drunk wine without toasting to something first.

He raised his glass and sipped. The desirable woman seated across from him seemed, literally, to glow with sensual promise. The wine, tainted by his frustration, tasted bittersweet. *We should be toasting the love we're about to make, the pleasure we're about to share. What would you taste like, Miss Brigitte Dumont? Would you be bittersweet, too?*

"Do you have any ideas about the mystery scenario yet?" she asked brightly.

The mystery scenario was the furthest thing from his mind. "Nothing beyond a murder," he replied. "I wanted to wait until I met the players."

"Rachel Wilkes is making us a body. Soft sculpture is her hobby."

"Soft sculpture?"

"Life-size rag dolls. She's waiting for the specifics."

"What kind of specifics?"

Brigitte smiled. "It would help if Rachel knew whether the victim is going to be male or female. There's a difference, you know."

"Really?"

"You hadn't noticed?"

"How anatomically precise are her dolls?"

"The men are taller than the women," Brigitte said dryly.

"Tell her to make the doll tall. Fuzz has never worked a female homicide. He prefers his women alive and breathing."

"Heavily," Brigitte murmured.

"Beg your pardon?"

"I said Fuzz seems to like his women breathing *heavily.*"

Charlie cocked an eyebrow. "Was that a note of feminist censure I heard, Miss Dumont?"

"I don't like seeing women portrayed as mindless bimbos who answer to the name of Babycakes."

"Ouch!" Charlie said amused.

Brigitte's mouth firmed into a petulant line.

Charlie grinned. "Lighten up, Babycakes. It's only a comic strip."

"Don't call me that!"

"I'm just getting into the mood for the mystery weekend. You have to be Babycakes in the scenario, you know."

"I do?" she asked skeptically.

"You're the logical choice. Your nieces are too young, and all the other Dumont women are married, with husbands very much in attendance. That leaves you, Babycakes."

"I told you not to call me that. And I'm not sure I can..."

"Of course you can! It can't be too difficult acting like a—what was it you said?—a mindless bimbo, and breathing heavily."

"It'll be a stretch."

"I don't know why," Charlie said, leveling his gaze a few inches below her chin. "I'll bet you've got great lungs."

"My lungs—" Brigitte began, but her pronouncement was cut short by a spurt of sharp squeals emanating from her handbag.

Charlie eyed the purse warily. "Holding an extraterrestrial hostage in there?"

"It's my *beeper*," Brigitte explained, madly digging in her purse to find it. Switching it off, she announced, "I've got to call the desk."

She dialed, identified herself and listened to the voice on the other end. From the expression on her face, Charlie surmised that whatever she was hearing was less than thrilling. Eventually she crisply thanked the person on the line for taking the message, and hung up.

IT WAS STEPHEN DUMONT who answered Charlie's knock at the door of Jean-Pierre and Marguerite's suite. After introducing himself, he ushered Charlie into the living room. To his surprise, Charlie found himself the center of attention.

Stephen first introduced Donna Prescott, the reporter, who occupied a floral-print wing chair. Then he presented the members of his family, one by one. Jean-Pierre

Dumont reigned over his clan from a thronelike leather recliner. Marguerite Dumont, youthful-looking for a matriarch, sat on the sofa with her daughter, Claire, and son-in-law, Claude. Brigitte and her nieces, Jennifer and Nicole, had dragged in wooden chairs from the dining-room suite, placed them next to the sofa.

"And of course, my wife, Janet," Stephen finished, smiling down at a lovely and pronouncedly pregnant woman in a love seat. He motioned for Charlie to sit as he joined Janet on the love seat.

Charlie sat down in the overstuffed armchair opposite the sofa, which obviously had been reserved for him. A lull in the conversation made the room seem too quiet, and Charlie was uncomfortably aware of the scrutiny of the Dumonts. They were curious, naturally, about the mystery scenario.

Brigitte's sister, Claire, quickly fired off the first volley. "Can you tell us anything about the murder-mystery plot, now that you've met us?"

The sister-in-law, Janet, backed her up. "We're all *so* curious about the parts we'll be playing."

"I have a few ideas," Charlie ventured. "But they're pretty sketchy."

The reporter, Donna, leaned forward slightly to offer tactful reinforcement. "A general idea would be helpful for the article."

Brigitte noted with wry amusement that Donna had punctuated her statement with body language that indicated more than a professional interest in her interview subject; and also that C. H. Battle appeared oblivious to her overtures. Of course, no reasonable man would flirt under the close perusal of a family of strangers who were pressing him for information.

"I want to be Babycakes," Nicole announced, in a voice meant to sound sultry and seductive. She was seated on the very edge of the wooden chair, with her chin tilted at a provocative angle and her chest thrust out.

Brigitte noted on second glance that Nicole's chest thrust forward of its own accord. *Been emptying the sock drawer into her training bra again,* she thought.

Brigitte wasn't the only one who noticed. Nicole's father, Claude, frowned at his wife. "Your daughter watches too much television."

"You're too young to be Babycakes," Jennifer informed her older sister.

"I am not!" Nicole turned to meet Charlie's gaze in challenge. "Am I?"

"Oh...but..." Charlie stammered, an expression of sheer horror on his face.

Brigitte took pity and rescued him. "Sorry, Nicole. Babycakes is already cast."

Nicole sighed woefully. "I should have known *you'd* get to do it. *You* get to do everything fun."

"That's enough, Nicole," Claire said with motherly menace.

Nicole set her jaw and slumped sullenly in her chair.

"We'll have to make you an important witness," Charlie said, grinning pure charm.

Nicole thawed visibly. "A witness?"

"You can see something or discover something that unlocks the entire mystery."

"Can I be a witness, too?" Jennifer asked.

Charlie nodded. "You and your sister can see something together."

"But—" Nicole's protest was cut off by a scowl from her mother.

Jennifer's face colored with excitement. "A witness," she said with a sigh. Then, turning to her mother, she asked, "Can I ask him now?"

Claire gave a gentle nod and Jennifer turned to Charlie. "We've been saving *Fantasy Fuzz* all week. Will you sign our papers?"

"Sure," Charlie agreed, clearly relieved that the request was a simple one.

Jennifer sprang up to go after the comic strips. As she passed Charlie's chair, he gave her a conspiratorial wink and stopped her with a *pssst* sound and a jerk of his head, then crooked his finger to indicate that she should lean over so he could whisper something in her ear. Seconds later, she straightened and walked away with a canary-feather-in-her-mouth grin.

Brigitte thought wryly that the acerbic Mr. Battle could turn on a lot of charm when he chose to.

"We'll work your pregnancy into the story line somehow," Charlie was telling Janet.

"What about the victim?" Donna asked.

"We have to create a character everyone would like to murder," Charlie said. "All the players need a motive in order to be suspect." He gave Brigitte a smoldering gaze. "We'll cook up a boyfriend for Babycakes, here. A fiancé, perhaps."

"Philandering, of course," Brigitte said dryly.

Donna turned to Brigitte. "That makes you the key suspect."

"You'll have to seduce Fantasy," Nicole suggested, and both her parents gasped.

"Far too much television," Claude muttered.

"I don't think . . ." Brigitte said. No one noticed that the thought went unfinished as Jennifer returned carrying a folded newspaper, a flat, heavy book and a stack of hotel stationery.

She held a felt-tip pen in the air and asked Charlie, "Is this okay?"

"It's just right," he told her, settling the book on his knees and centering a sheet of the stationery on it. Everyone watched with rapt attention as he caricatured Jennifer, rendering her likeness as a *Fantasy Fuzz* character. Jennifer squealed with delight when he put the now famous C. H. Battle signature in the bottom corner of the page and then handed it to her.

"Do me!" Nicole said, striking her siren pose again.

Charlie sketched with impressive speed. The resulting image was Nicole, but older and more sophisticated. He captioned it *Babycakes 2010*.

Nicole glowed with pride as he passed it to her.

"Any other customers?" Charlie asked, scanning faces.

Donna gasped. "Would you? I promise to frame it and hang it in my office."

"The girl reporter," Charlie mused, as he propelled his pen into motion again. The result was Donna in a trench coat, a reporter's tablet in her hand.

"Do Grandpère and Grandmère," Jennifer urged.

Charlie proceeded to capture Jean-Pierre's zest for life and his wife's quiet charm.

Stephen and Janet were next—Stephen, robust and full of energy; Janet, vivacious and very much pregnant. Then Claude and Claire were depicted as serious, with a hint of mischief.

"And now Aunt Brigitte," Jennifer coaxed. She had moved close to Charlie's chair and was leaning against the back, watching him work.

Charlie grinned almost menacingly at Brigitte. "Ah, yes. Babycakes." He noted the sudden stiffening of her spine, the sharp inhalation of breath as though she were steeling herself for a fate worse than death. Perversely, he drew her exactly as he would draw a Babycakes character in his strip, exaggerating that crooked smile and making the V at the neck of her blouse plunge lower than in reality to reveal a more ample cleavage than nature had actually supplied to Brigitte Dumont.

"Radical!" Nicole exclaimed approvingly. "Aunt Brigitte, he made you sexy."

Charlie shrugged sheepishly. "An artist draws truth, eh?"

"And a cartoonist draws cartoons," Brigitte added. *If it wasn't for BARF—*

"Some people think that cartoonists are the real chroniclers," Donna said. She intercepted the drawing as Charlie offered it to Brigitte. "We're going to need artwork with the story. May I run this?"

"But, it's—" Brigitte protested.

"Pure *Fantasy Fuzz*," Donna explained. "With C. H. Battle's signature." She looked at Charlie. "May we use it? I might be able to make the editor cough up an art fee, although it would just be a token."

"Take it," Charlie told her, noting the vexed expression on Brigitte's face. "And send the art fee to BARF in my name."

Realizing she was trapped, Brigitte swallowed hard. To refuse to let them run the cartoon, denying BARF both the free space in *Contemporary Canada* and the artist's fee Charlie was donating to the fund, would be petty.

"Did Brigitte tell me you were wearing a Fantasy Fuzz bombardier jacket tonight?" Donna asked Charlie.

Charlie nodded.

"I'd like to photograph you in it. It might be easier before Family Night gets under way."

"Whatever you say," Charlie replied.

"Great!" Donna stuffed her reporter's notebook into her purse and gathered her camera equipment. She looked at Brigitte. "How about you, Babycakes?"

"Oh, no!" Brigitte shook her head in emphasis. "I didn't . . . I'm not dressed for the part."

"You're fine!" Donna insisted. "We'll just unbutton your top button. Babycakes and Fantasy Fuzz. It'll make a great publicity shot."

*"Unbutton?"* Brigitte parroted hoarsely.

"It's for BARF," Charlie said.

"Yes, Brigitte," Stephen prompted. "It's for BARF. You've got to give your all."

"A Dumont can do no less for a worthy cause," her father drawled.

Brigitte glared at him as though he'd just sold his baby daughter into white slavery. "My own father!"

"We're talking a simple button, not a bordello, eh?" Jean-Pierre countered.

"Jean-Pierre!" his wife protested.

Donna stood and heaved the strap of her camera bag over her shoulder. "Ready?" she asked, turning from Charlie to Brigitte.

Brigitte threw up her hands in supplication. "Guess we'll see you guys in the dining room," she told her family. "I'm off to preserve the Dumont family honor. What's a button in the face of dishonor?"

In Charlie's suite, Donna exclaimed over the view while Charlie put on his jacket. "It's perfect," she said. "A perfect backdrop for the photo. It'll fix the characters in Banff immediately." Positioning Brigitte in front of the scenic window, she poked a light meter toward her.

Brigitte tried to emulate some of her friend's enthusiasm, but was too preoccupied. She had no problems with performing for audiences—never had—but the prospect of posing as a femme fatale in the suite for the benefit of one camera was daunting.

Charlie had put on the jacket and was standing nearby, waiting for directions and looking even more self-conscious than she felt. Donna, who'd been adjusting knobs and dials on her camera and strobe, looked up as though she'd suddenly remembered that Charlie and Brigitte were in the room, then turned her attention to Charlie. She straightened the collar of his jacket unnecessarily, letting her hand linger on his shoulder as she tilted her head, appraising man and jacket.

What had failed for Nicole worked for Donna, Brigitte thought with a stab of something in the general neighborhood of jealousy. Donna was no precocious child who watched too much television; she was a woman who understood the game. Brigitte took grim satisfaction in the fact that, as before, C. H. Battle seemed not to notice that he was being asked to play. He seemed, if anything, to be wooden with apprehension about the photo shoot.

Donna walked him to the window and turned his body at an angle to it. "Relax!" she said. "It's a camera, not an Uzi." Stepping back, she lifted her camera to her eye and turned some more dials. "Good," she said, and hit the self-propelling shutter.

The camera clack-clack-clacked through half a dozen rapid exposures before she released the button. "Great! Now, Brigitte, step in next to him. Good. Turn your body at the same angle from the window as his. Yes. Good." She lowered the camera and sighed. "The button, Brigitte. Yes. Fold back your collar. That's perfect. Now, Fantasy, give her one of those looks...."

*As if he had to be told!* Between the sun beating against the glass, the leather jacket and watching Brigitte undo the top button of her blouse, Charlie was more than a little hot under the collar. And he was having one heck of a time just looking.

Brigitte felt her face suffuse with heat. C. H. Battle could melt a thirty-foot bank of packed snow with those eyes. It was bad enough having to undo her top button with him watching, but to have to stand there while he looked as though he might devour her at any moment while Donna watched through the viewfinder—Donna, who'd been flirting with him moments earlier...

The camera clicked—five, six, seven times—then ground to silence. "We need some action now," Donna said.

"Action?" Brigitte croaked.

"Okay, Fantasy, you're the writer—what would Baby-cakes do in this scenario?"

"She'd . . ." Charlie replied, his voice hoarse as he tried to concentrate on the question. He swallowed. "If she were a suspect, she'd be trying to distract him."

"You heard the man, Brigitte. Distract, distract."

Something in Brigitte snapped. *Distract him? He wanted to be distracted? She'd show him distraction!* "You mean like this?" she purred, putting her hands on his shoulders and leaning close enough for her thigh to graze his. Tilting her head back, she gave him back some of the sensuality he'd been oozing.

*Go ahead, devour me,* her eyes challenged. *Taste me,* teased her slightly parted lips. Her chest rose noticeably as her breathing deepened, and her thigh pressed almost imperceptibly closer to his so that the heat from their bodies mingled.

"Attagirl, Brigitte," Donna said. "Turn it on! Your move now, Fantasy."

*His move?* Charlie was immobilized by the powerful need to taste her. She was only acting, he knew; performing for the camera in a role he'd assigned her. So why was his heart hammering? Why did the blood it pushed through his body seem hotter than usual? Did Fantasy go through all this?

*Fantasy.* What *would* Fantasy do? How would he deal with Brigitte Dumont's seductive overtures?

*Kiss her, stupid!* Charlie told himself, picturing a cartoon panel of Fantasy Fuzz with Babycakes Brigitte writhing in his arms.

The thought of Brigitte Dumont writhing—along with the scent of her perfume that tortured him with each intake of breath—drove him over the edge of control.

# 3

IT WAS FANTASY FUZZ who reached for Brigitte, Fantasy Fuzz's hand that looped her sleek ponytail around his hand and tugged, urging her head back as he moved his face closer to hers. It was Fantasy Fuzz who growled as he slid his free arm across her waist to jerk her body against his just before he pressed his lips to hers.

But it was Charlie Battle whose entire sensory system reeled with the taste and feel of Brigitte Dumont. And it was Brigitte Dumont who felt herself melting into the aggressive embrace, Brigitte Dumont whose lips swelled and parted under the pressure of Charlie Battle's hungry mouth.

Fantasy had not prepared Charlie for the reality of Brigitte Dumont. She was soft yet firm, solid yet pliant; small compared to his own hulking size but, oh, so substantial a presence in his arms. He burned where her body touched his, but he only wanted the flame to grow hotter.

Brigitte hadn't known that sexual chemistry could be so volatile; hadn't realized that the smoldering looks that had made her uncomfortable all afternoon were simply foreplay for this explosive touching. At first she was stunned by his rough demands, then thrilled as the hand coiled in her hair became caressing, and the arm that anchored her to him turned from unyielding steel to a firm embrace, and demand softened into request.

"Yo! Babycakes! Detective Fuzz!" Donna's voice seemed to come from afar. "Brigitte! *Cut!*"

Guiltily, Brigitte jerked away from Battle, as the sound of her name jarred her back to reality. When had she put her arms around Battle's neck, woven her fingers into his hair? Her breath coming in labored inhalations, she stared at Donna, feeling as though she'd just emerged from a fog.

Charlie suffered Brigitte's lurch away from him as both a physical ache and a rebuke. What had happened between them left him enervated and embarrassed. She had goaded, tempted, dared; and he'd allowed himself to respond with force, vulnerability and bravado.

Fuzz! He'd gotten caught up in his own cartoon supermacho man. Fuzz would have behaved the same way and not been embarrassed or defensive. Fuzz would know how to handle the situation.

Frantically Charlie imagined a cartoon panel—there they were, Fuzz and Babycakes standing in front of the reporter with their chests heaving. He saw the speech balloon, mentally filled in Fantasy's ego-salvaging dialogue. Then he turned to Donna and quipped: "Get what you needed, Babycakes?"

Brigitte felt her already-hot face flame with sudden rage. After kissing her like a lusty sailor who'd just come ashore after ten years at sea—in front of a camera, no less—the insensitive macho clod was calling the next most convenient woman Babycakes!

"Get what I needed?" Donna said incredulously. "The film ran out and you guys just kept on. My lenses are fogged from the steam!"

"Good," Charlie mumbled. Though he wanted to very badly, he deliberately avoided looking at Brigitte. He wasn't sure what he'd do if her face told him she'd been as affected by the kiss as he, although he was certain it wouldn't be appropriate for an audience or a pictorial essay in *Contemporary Canada*. Or worse, if she were gloating over having taunted him into making a jackass of himself, he didn't think he could bear seeing that in her eyes.

"Damn!" Donna said, wrestling with a knob on the tripod she was collapsing. "This bolt won't budge. Would you . . . ?"

Relieved to have an excuse to move and something other than Brigitte on which to focus his attention, Charlie sprinted the six feet to the tripod and gave the knob a savage twist. The tripod collapsed with a crash, and Charlie and Donna both leaped to pick it up and put it right. They looked as if they were wrestling with a space alien.

Brigitte sensed the prospect of escape. "There are some loose ends I have to tie up for Family Night. I'll see you in the dining room." Before either could reply, she swept past them.

The elevator arrived quickly and was empty. Brigitte stepped in and sighed with relief as the doors closed. Out of habit, she turned to the mirrored side-wall to check her appearance, and was shocked by what she saw. Her hands flew to her cheeks, still flushed from . . . the hottest kiss she'd ever experienced with her clothes on? Embarrassment? Rage?

A ragged sigh tore from her throat. *All of the above.*

Brigitte was no amateur when it came to kissing. She'd been kissed by men from at least half the nations of the free world. She could distinguish natural talent from technique, and art wasn't the only talent with which C. H. Battle had been blessed in abundance.

Why did a man who could kiss like that have to be such a turkey? Calling her Babycakes. Drawing her with more *cleavage* than the Rocky Mountains. Kissing her senseless one minute, then, as if the kiss hadn't fazed him, calling another woman Babycakes the next.

She fumed again at the thought of it. If she had to be cast in the role of Babycakes for the mystery weekend, drawn as a top-heavy sex symbol and kissed—mauled!—in front of a camera, was it unreasonable to expect exclusive rights to the part?

JEAN-PIERRE DUMONT gave his watch a glance. "Our guest of honor is cutting it close, Brigitte. Are you certain he knows what time he is expected?"

"He knows, Père," Brigitte answered. "He and Donna are probably still talking. She was planning on pumping him for details."

For her own reasons, Brigitte was just as anxious about C. H. Battle's imminent arrival. She gazed around the Chalet Dumont dining room. No sign of Battle. *At least*, she thought, *he'll have no trouble finding our table*. On Family Night, they traditionally occupied a table positioned midway between the side wall and the center of the room. Designed to hold ten people comfortably, the round table could, in a pinch, accommodate up to a dozen. Tonight, Brigitte had ordered it set for eleven, to include the nine Dumonts and their two guests, C. H. Battle and Donna Prescott. Except for her mother, who was playing dinner music on the piano, the rest of her family were all present.

Stephen, seated on Brigitte's right, said, "Donna looked ready and willing to pump him for more than a story."

"That's just Donna," Brigitte replied. "She has a bad case of celebrity drool. She's earning kudos at work for having snared an exclusive with Mr. Elusive."

"Mr. Battle didn't seem too interested," Janet remarked.

"He was too busy oggling Babycakes, here," Stephen said.

Brigitte rolled her eyes in exasperation. "Don't call me that."

"What's going on with you and our special guest?"

Brigitte felt her cheeks getting warm until she realized there was no way Stephen could have heard about the photo session that almost went X-rated. "Going on?"

"You don't usually insult our guests."

"Insult?"

Stephen turned to Janet. "My baby sister is playing innocent. She used to do this when we were children so I would get in trouble and she wouldn't."

"It always worked, too."

"Stop trying to change the subject," Stephen countered. "The man referred to himself as an artist, and you called him a cartoonist."

Brigitte sniffed disdainfully. "You saw that *picture* he did of me!"

"I'm surprised you didn't like that picture, Brigitte. I thought you wanted more—" He gestured with his hands in front of his chest. "You know."

He turned to Janet. "She used to moan and groan because she was too flat." His voice went falsetto. "'I look like a pancake. My shirts look like a boy's wearing them.'"

"That was a long time ago," Brigitte protested, and glanced down at her chest before adding, lamely, "I've grown since then. Besides, big boobs don't age well. They sag."

"So at least you don't have to have gray hairs *and* sagging boobs, eh?" Stephen teased.

"Speaking of bosoms," Janet said, leaning forward to speak to Brigitte in a confidential tone, "is it my imagination or has Nicole been expanding and shrinking before our very eyes?"

Brigitte glanced quickly to the opposite side of the table. Jennifer was engaged in a spirited discussion with her grandfather, and Nicole was hunched in her chair pouting. Claire's face had the tortured expression of a mother trapped in a no-matter-what-you-do-it's-wrong parental warp.

"I think Claire and Nicole put away some laundry before coming downstairs," Brigitte answered Janet. "The only socks Nicole is wearing now are the ones inside her sneakers."

"Poor Nicole," Janet said.

"Poor Claire," Stephen said with a sigh. Patting Janet's swollen abdomen, he asked, "Are you sure we're ready for this?"

"No," Janet replied, giving him a smile that oozed intimacy. "But I'm pretty sure it's too late to change our minds, so we're just going to have to cope."

Watching the glow of this exchange, Brigitte felt left out and, although she tried to fight it, a bit resentful over Stephen's defection to his bride. Although she liked her sister-in-law, Brigitte was still adjusting to having to share her older brother after his whirlwind courtship and sudden marriage.

Claire had married when Brigitte was still a child, so it seemed natural to Brigitte that Claire's attention should be focused primarily on Claude and their children. But it wasn't so easy to adapt to being the outsider around Stephen and his wife. Brigitte felt stuck, alone, between generations. In an occasional morose moment, it seemed to her that around the chalet lately it was her mom and dad, Claire and Claude, Stephen and Janet, Jennifer and Nicole, and herself and *nobody*. And with her nieces leaping into adolescence and her brother's wife blossoming with child, Brigitte heard her biological clock ticking away like an overwound watch.

The arrival of Battle and Donna created a **stir** at the table as Jean-Pierre stood to greet them and pull out a chair for Donna next to his own. That left the seat next to Brigitte for Charlie.

She was immediately aware of his presence as he settled his large frame into the chair and his biceps brushed her upper arm, radiating male warmth. Their gazes met and held a second too long before Battle greeted her with a nod and she acknowledged it with an answering tilt of her chin, then turned away to escape the unresolved business between them. She breathed easier when Stephen commented on Battle's Fantasy Fuzz jacket, initiating a conversation that kept them occupied until Claire caught her attention and lifted an eyebrow to indicate that they should get the entertainment segment of Family Night under way.

Family Night at the Chalet Dumont had begun years earlier with impromptu piano-playing by Marguerite Dumont on Mondays—the après-ski combo's night off. Gradually her daughter joined the act, telling homespun, hokey vaudevillian jokes and leading sing-alongs. Through time, Family Night evolved into a Banff institution, when the local residents would gather in the chalet dining room to see how outrageous the marginally talented but effervescent Dumont girls could get.

The stage was centered on the rear wall of the room between two sets of swing doors that opened out from the service hall. A small dance floor stretched out in front of the stage. Tonight Brigitte, her sister Claire and their father skirted the edge of the dance floor as they walked the short distance from table to stage. Brigitte stood silently beside Jean-Pierre, as he, the consummate innkeeper, welcomed the chalet guests warmly and introduced first his wife, still at the piano, then Brigitte and Claire, who were waiting to start the Family Night chitchat. He paused at the piano to kiss his wife on the cheek before returning to the family table.

"Well, Brigitte," Claire opened, "we have something really special to talk about tonight, don't we?"

"Sure do," Brigitte said. "I want to talk about Mortie and Bernie."

Claire feigned surprise. "You mean Saint Moritz and Bern, our dogs?"

"Yep."

"You all know Mortie and Bernie, don't you, folks?" Claire continued, then paused for the smattering of applause at the mention of the gentle Saint Bernards who were favorites of the chalet guests. She turned back to Brigitte. "Why do you want to talk about Mortie and Bernie?"

"Well," Brigitte replied, "I always knew Mortie and Bernie were pretty."

Claire acknowledged this with a stage nod, while murmurs of agreement came from the audience.

"And I always knew they were friendly."

"Yes, they're friendly," Claire agreed.

"Well, I never realized until this afternoon how smart they are." Brigitte let the statement hang in the air for effect.

Claire, playing straight man, finally asked, "What makes you think Mortie and Bernie are smart?"

"I was watching them play, listening to them talk to each other...."

"Wait a minute, Brigitte. Dogs don't talk."

"Bernie and Mortie do," Brigitte replied. "That's how I found out how smart they are. Do you know what they said to each other?"

Claire rolled her eyes. "I'm afraid to ask."

"They said, 'BARF.'"

"All dogs say barf. It's called barking."

"Nope," Brigitte said, shaking her head. "They didn't say barf. They said BARF. In capital letters."

"Ohhhh," Claire said. "You mean the acronym BARF."

"That's right. *B-A-R-F.* It stands for the Banff Area Recycling Foundation."

Grinning at her sister, Claire told her in a stage aside, "That's sneaky, sis."

From his seat at the Dumont family table, Charlie watched Brigitte shrug prettily, ingratiatingly. With such a shrug—so utterly female—and such bright-eyed guile-lessness, he thought, a woman could get away with fel-ony crimes. It was the attitude he tried to capture in his Babycakes sketches. *Honest, officer, I didn't know ar-senic dissolved in coffee was fatal. I was just trying to clean the coffeepot.*

He couldn't keep his eyes off Brigitte. Her dark hair shone under the spotlight and her skin seemed almost to glow. She appeared comfortable in that spotlight; at ease, as though being center stage were her due for having been born a Dumont. She seemed to be enjoying performing as much as he was dreading his imminent introduction. His gut constricted at the thought of getting up in front of this crowd, of being applauded because he was C. H. Battle, creator of *Fantasy Fuzz*. He'd never get used to it—to the celebrity, to the way the public clamored after someone famous.

Much of his adult life had been spent in a garret, cre-ating imaginary people with pen and ink. For years those doodles had peopled his world, and he'd been the only person who cared about them. He had an entire wall lined with rejection slips explaining that one character was in-triguing but just wouldn't have a broad enough appeal, while another showed promise but just wasn't quite orig-inal enough in concept, and yet another was too abrasive to be sympathetic. His characters, like their creator, went unnoticed—until one editor took a chance on a chauvin-istic homicide detective and the public embraced Fuzz.

"We all know that we should recycle," Brigitte was say-ing.

"We recycle a lot of jokes around here on Family Night," Claire interjected, drawing titters from the crowd.

Brigitte harrumphed daintily. "Yes, well . . . I'm afraid *that* recycling doesn't do a lot to help the ecology."

"They, uh, do get a little overripe, sometimes." Claire earned full laughs this time as she pinched her nostrils together with her fingertips.

"Let's get serious a minute, Claire. The fact is, most people want to recycle, but there aren't enough recycling centers in Alberta to handle all those old newspapers and bottles and cans."

"And that's why there's BARF."

"That's right. BARF would like to establish a recycling-processing center in the area."

"That sounds like an ecological idea. And I understand you and BARF are planning something...."

"Plotting."

"I beg your pardon?"

"We're not just planning, we're plotting," Brigitte said drolly. "Murder!"

"Murder?"

"Are you hard-of-hearing tonight?"

"I must be. I thought I just heard you say you and BARF were plotting a murder."

"That's right," Brigitte answered smugly, grinning at the audience. "Murder. Right here at the Chalet Dumont. We're going to have a body, and all kinds of suspects, and..."

"Ohhhh," Claire said, nodding comprehension. "You mean a murder-mystery weekend, where the guests all play detective and try to figure out 'whodunit.'"

"Yep! But our guests for this weekend are going to have some very special help."

"Special help?"

"Yep. And I'll give you a hint." Brigitte paused to build suspense. "Babycakes!"

A murmur of excitement passed through the crowd.

"You don't mean?" Claire said.

Brigitte nodded. "Detective Fantasy Fuzz is going to be here to catch the perpetrator."

"But Fantasy Fuzz is a cartoon character."

"Ah!" Brigitte panned the audience with a canary-feathers-in-her-mouth grin. "But we have someone very special to play Fantasy Fuzz—Fantasy's creator, Mr. C. H. Battle." She extended an arm in Charlie's direction. "Mr. Battle, come on up."

Charlie clenched his jaw to keep from scowling as he rose from his chair. He'd hoped just to stand, bob his head at the crowd and sit down, but she was calling him up to the platform, putting him on display. He'd be expected to smile, of course, although smiling was the last thing he felt like doing in front of a roomful of gawking people.

He wasn't used to the gawking—never would get used to it. Did they expect to see the wheels of creativity working in his mind, or look at his hands and see some physical evidence of artistic ability? He suspected they weren't really seeing him as a human being, but were actually searching for Fantasy Fuzz: *Move over, Dr. Frankenstein. You're not the only one who created an unwieldy monster.*

He reached the small stage. Brigitte and Claire stood on either side of him. Brigitte said into the microphone, expansively, "Ladies and gentlemen, Alberta's own Mr. C. H. Battle, creator of the *Fantasy Fuzz* comic strip."

The applause of the audience embarrassed him. He felt like an absolute fool standing there like a trained chimpanzee on exhibit. But then Brigitte looped her arm through his, and embarrassment was superseded by the awareness of her body brushing his. It was show business, he knew—the chummy camaraderie of performers sharing a stage. But that didn't make her body any less real or less warm—and it didn't stop his own body from responding to the touch of hers.

"Mr. Battle," she said, although she looked straight out at the crowd instead of at him, "you're a charter member of BARF, aren't you?"

Charlie stared at the microphone she'd thrust under his nose for a couple of seconds before gathering his wits to reply. "Yes."

"In fact, few people realize it, but a few years back, you won BARF's annual poster-design contest, didn't you?"

Charlie nodded affirmatively. *Nodded!* Brigitte couldn't believe how wooden he was. He certainly wasn't making her job easy with his nods and one-word responses.

"Why don't you tell us a little about that poster," she persisted.

"It was a cartoon sketch of a tree trying to talk a lumberjack out of chopping him down."

He was deadly sincere, but the audience heard wry wit and responded with chuckles. Brigitte heaved a sigh of relief that the interview was no longer falling flat. She looked past Charlie to her sister, who'd stepped off the stage and was holding the edge of a piece of fabric draped over an easel. "Claire," she said, nodding gravely.

Claire yanked away the drape to reveal a framed poster and sang, "Ta-da!"

"Thank you! This is the original poster submitted to BARF by C. H. Battle, with his signature. And the exciting news is . . ." She turned to her mother. "A little fanfare, please!"

Mrs. Dumont complied with an appropriate keyboard trill.

"You could own this original C. H. Battle poster! BARF is auctioning it off during the BARF Death at the Dumont Mystery Weekend."

"Mr. Battle's not only going to play Fantasy Fuzz," Claire told the audience. "He's also going to write the mystery scenario for the entire weekend."

Brigitte batted her eyes at Charlie. "You really get into murder, don't you?"

Charlie looked into her deceptively innocent face. Was she deliberately goading him? Or merely bantering for the audience? Either way, he was not a man prone to witty ad-lib, and found himself without a clever comeback.

Before anyone noticed his silence, Claire piped in. "The Dumonts are all going to be suspects."

Brigitte didn't hold grudges—she got even. Her ego still stinging from the episode in Charlie's suite, she recognized the perfect opportunity to exact a little revenge—to give C. H. Battle a dose of his own medicine; to dish out to the gander what he'd fed to the goose.

Extricating her right arm from his, she raised it to his shoulder, then traced his collarbone to his neck with a sensual brush of her forefinger. When her hand reached his neck, she curled her fingers over his nape, cradling it. Tilting her head so she could see his face, she rested her ear against his chest and gave him an adoring, come-hither look.

A smattering of oohs and ahs from the audience emboldened her. Bending her left knee, she twisted her body and pressed her thigh across the front of his thighs and wiggled her upper body against his.

Amid more oohs from the audience, Claire said, "Brigitte?"

Brigitte lifted her head from Charlie's chest and smiled innocently. "I'm practicing."

"We know which part Brigitte got," Claire quipped.

Titters grew into full laughter. The audience was eating it up. Brigitte snapped back into character, flashing moon eyes at Charlie's face. She moved the microphone close to her lips, which were practically touching Charlie's breastbone, and, plunging her fingers upward into Charlie's hair, sighed, moaning, "Oh, Fantasy."

Claire cleared her throat meaningfully into her microphone. "Ahem. I hate to interrupt, but the Chalet Dumont *is* a family-oriented establishment."

Feigning resignation, Brigitte stepped away from Charlie and cooed into the microphone, "Later, Fantasy."

The audience clapped rowdily.

"Well," Claire said, "that's just a preview of the fun we're going to have at the Death at the Dumont Mystery Weekend, with Mr. C. H. Battle playing his cartoon detective Fantasy Fuzz and Brigitte playing Babycakes. Right now, though, my daughters, Nicole and Jennifer—wave, girls, so we know where you are—are out there among you. Jennifer is passing out song sheets for our Family Night sing-along, and Nicole has Chalet Dumont kazoos for sale."

Brigitte took over the commentary. "The newest Dumont, our sister-in-law, Janet, started a kazoo tradition last year, and every Monday night we sell the kazoos for those of you who can't sing but who don't want to miss out on the fun."

"Not that singing well has ever been a requirement for a Chalet Dumont sing-along," Claire added.

"Tonight, in honor of Mr. C. H. Battle's visit to the Chalet Dumont and his many contributions of time and talent to BARF, we're donating all the profits from the kazoo sales to BARF."

"In a moment, Janet and her legendary kazoo are going to kick off the sing-along with a very special song. For the time being, Mama is going to play something soothing." Claire stretched her arm out toward the piano. "Ladies and gentlemen, Marguerite Dumont at the keyboard!"

As her mother launched into a medley of Swing Era classics, Brigitte switched off the microphone. She turned to speak to Battle and found only his back to her as he prepared to step off the stage. Grabbing a handful of leather from the wide back of his jacket, she said, "Not so fast, big guy!"

She was almost sorry she'd stopped him when he spun around and she saw the expression on his face. She thought she'd scored a direct hit with her Babycakes routine, and his scowl confirmed it. Refusing to be intimidated, she swallowed the lump in her throat, jutted her chin defiantly and told him, "We still need you onstage."

Charlie snuffled disdainfully, "Is that a fact?"

"We're going to sing a special song in your honor."

She was giving him that doe-eyed, innocent look. Charlie set his jaw in irritation. She was good at "innocent," he'd give her that; she made him want to believe that she was as guileless as she appeared. But his body was still humming with the memory of her thigh pressed over his, and the lingering effect on his senses only made him more aware of his vulnerability where she was concerned. She might slip in and out of character as easily as breathing, but Charlie Battle found it a little tough pretending to be a cartoon personality when he had a delectable female human body pressed against him. She might be able to turn the seduction act on and off like water from a spigot, but his body didn't flip-flop from fantasy to reality that easily—no matter what his mind was telling it. Fantasy Fuzz might have coolly handled being onstage with Babycakes Dumont, but Charlie Battle was more than a little hot under the collar from the experience. The only thing on his mind at the moment besides Brigitte Dumont was *escape*.

"I can listen from the table," he said.

"It'll be more fun if you're on the stage so we can sing to you." For a moment Brigitte thought he might balk, and the expression on his face was so anguished that if he had, she would have let him return to the table without arguing the point. Sometimes she forgot that some people were as intimidated by an audience as she was enlivened by one.

He seemed to deliberate over what to do, then heaved the sigh of a man sorely taxed by his lot in life but resigned to it. Brigitte instinctively reached out to reassure him. "It won't be so bad."

Charlie looked down at her hand. It stood out, pale against the crumpled brown leather of his jacket sleeve,

the fingers long and delicately tapered, the nails shaped
and polished. He recalled the riot of sensation those fingers had set off when they'd caressed his nape.

Gentle hands. Caressing fingers curled over his arm.
Charlie grew tense as he fortified himself against the al-
lure of Brigitte Dumont and her touch. He was too inex-
perienced with women to enter into casual liaisons. He
couldn't take women or romance lightly, whereas everything about Brigitte Dumont seemed to indicate that she
rarely took men or romance—or life in general—seriously.

He forced his eyes away from her hand and looked at her
face instead. It was a tactical error to look at that face,
risking the possibility that she might smile that slightly
crooked smile again and he'd be as beguiled by it as ever.
She did. And he was. And the warmth in her eyes reminded him of the fiery desire he'd seen there after their
kiss. "I think we've stirred up some interest in the murder
weekend," she said.

Fantasy Fuzz would have grinned at her lasciviously and
informed her that she'd stirred up more than that, but
Charlie just murmured a noncommittal, "Umm."

Claire and Janet had been working with the audio
equipment, checking to be sure the standing microphone
was set up properly for Janet's kazoo number. Content
that everything was in order, they approached Brigitte and
Charlie. "The song sheets are out and Nicole has finished
selling kazoos. As soon as Mom wraps up this song . . ."

Brigitte nodded and, looping her arm around Charlie's
again, positioned him between herself and Claire, while
Janet went to the standing mike. Seconds later, Claire was
introducing Janet and inviting all the nonsingers who'd
bought or brought kazoos to join in the kazoo chorus.

"You've heard of heavy-metal music," she said. "Well,
the Chalet Dumont is into light-metal music. Now, all of
you Dumont kazooers raise those kazoos in the air. Let us

see them. Excellent. Our special song tonight is about our special guest, Mr. C. H. Battle, creator of *Fantasy Fuzz*, and we'll be singing it to the tune of 'Clementine.' Mom's playing the melody now, just to refresh your memory."

Brigitte took up the commentary. "In order to allow our honored guest to be part of our tribute, Nicole has a special presentation."

Nicole, who'd been waiting silently at the edge of the platform, came forward. Claire held out her microphone so her daughter could speak to Charlie. "Mr. Battle, we'd like you to have this kazoo so you can be an honorary member of the Chalet Dumont Kazooers."

Charlie smiled at Nicole as he accepted the kazoo, and thanked her.

As Nicole backed away, Claire said, wildly enthusiastically, "All right, all you Dumont kazooers..." She turned to Charlie. "And honorary kazooers. Prepare... to... toot!"

"Kazoos in place!" Janet said, lifting her own kazoo to her mouth as Mrs. Dumont signaled the end of the chorus with a short fanfare. At the beginning of the new verse, Janet hummed into the metal instrument, producing a tinny melody recognizable as the traditional one being played on the piano. Across the dining room, other kazooers joined in, creating a respectable buzz.

Brigitte turned on her microphone, thrust it a few inches from Charlie's nose and gave him a prod in the ribs with her elbow. "Hum, kazooer!"

Feeling utterly foolish, Charlie hummed into the unfamiliar gadget, comforted that the honk he added to the din, despite being amplified, was scarcely distinguishable from the squeaks and rasps of the other amateur musicmakers.

Brigitte moved the microphone away quickly and gave his arm a reassuring squeeze. Their eyes met, and one corner of her mouth lifted briefly in an approving smile that made him forget his embarrassment. Then she turned her attention back to performing, humming into the mike. Despite being on the stage in front of a roomful of strangers, Charlie devoted his attention to enjoying the feel of Brigitte Dumont's body next to his.

His reprieve from humiliation was short-lived, however, for the kazoo chorus was quickly over, and Claire directed everyone to pick up their song sheets. "We're going to run through the chorus first, so all of you join in with us, either by voice or kazoo!"

After a tinkling trill from the piano, she led the audience in singing, accompanied by Janet's kazoo.

"In the comics, in the comics,
There's a cop we all respect . . ."

Running her hand over his chest, Brigitte crooned into the microphone: "Fantasy Fuzz!"
The audience concluded the chorus.

"Finding clues and stalking suspects,
He finds solutions we don't expect!"

"Now you know the chorus, let's take it verse by verse," Claire instructed.

"He's no wienie, he's a genius—
Perseverance is his game!"

"Never gives up!" Brigitte cooed this time.

"He's persistent,
And consistent,
And he always finds a dame."

"The chorus again, then verse two," Claire prompted.

"Calls her Babycakes,
Calls her Babycakes.
She seduces him, 'tis true—"

This time, Brigitte drew a circle around his ear with her fingertip as she purred. "So sad, but true!"

"He will kiss her,
But never miss her,
When he opens the next case."

Verse three was more of the same.

"Fan-ta-sy Fuzz,
Fan-ta-sy Fuzz,
He's a hero, strong and sure—"

"He's very sure!" Brigitte added suggestively.

"Catching killers,
Thwarting criminals,
He's a man whose heart is pure."

"Pure?" Brigitte asked, lifting her eyebrows skeptically as she eyed Charlie from head to toe. Then, shaking her head knowingly, she said, "Naw!"

The audience managed a hearty collective laugh before resuming the chorus, which ended in a grand finale that included a duet by Janet on the kazoo and her mother-in-law at the piano. Brigitte took over as the final notes faded, holding her arm out toward Charlie. "Ladies and gentlemen, the object of our affection and admiration, the subject of tonight's sing-along, Mr. C. H. Battle!"

In the midst of the thunderous applause that followed her cue, she took Charlie's hand in hers and squeezed it gently. "You're off the hook now," she whispered into his ear. "Thanks for being such a good sport."

The crowd had broken into a new song by the time Charlie reached his seat. Stephen Dumont welcomed him by picking up a bottle of wine that had been left on the table and gesturing toward the glass at Charlie's place to ask if Charlie would like him to fill it. Charlie nodded.

As Stephen leaned close enough to pour the wine, he said drolly, "Welcome to insanity, Dumont-style."

"You do this every Monday night?"

"To my everlasting embarrassment and consternation," Stephen replied. His eyes went to the stage, focusing on his wife, who was obliviously humming into her kazoo, and he shook his head gravely. "Janet was a perfectly normal, well-adjusted adult human being before I brought her here and my sisters corrupted her."

"You don't . . . sing or anything?"

"I'd sooner have my fingernails ripped off."

Charlie laughed aloud, and raised his glass in a salute to Stephen's refreshing candor—and sanity.

He'd barely taken his first sip of wine before the autograph seekers began to line up, wanting him to sign their song sheets.

The next time he had sufficient opportunity to take note of what was going on onstage, Claire was talking about a special request. She finished by looking at the family table. "Papa?"

Jean-Pierre stood and walked to the edge of the stage, arriving just in time to extend a hand to Brigitte as she stepped onto the dance floor. Claire handed her father and sister each a top hat and cane, and they donned the hats and positioned the canes in their hands with the expediency of drill-team members handling ornamental rifles.

From the stand-up mike, Janet said, "All right, ka-zooers, this is your last chance to hum along tonight! You all know the melody. Let's buzz!"

"Me and My Shadow." The old man and his daughter lined up and executed a synchronized soft-shoe routine to the old favorite, accompanied by Mrs. Dumont and the tinny chorus of kazoos. Charlie's eyes were drawn to Brigitte, who seemed brighter than humanly natural under the spotlights. She moved lithely, flowing comfortably through the steps of the routine. Charlie noticed every part of her—the smiling face peeping from under the brim of the hat, the slender body swaying gracefully in rhythm with the music, the pretty hands confidently maneuvering the cane.

Charlie watched, and remembered what it had been like to kiss her. He watched, and desired. He watched, and envied.

It was so easy for her. Greeting special guests, making them *feel* special. Performing under the lights. Sliding in and out of roles. It was her life and she was comfortable with it; comfortable, because it was the life to which she'd been born.

She was Jean-Pierre Dumont's daughter. He'd been a notorious playboy; she was a flirt. He was the consummate host, the innkeeper; she was the innkeeper's daughter, a consummate hostess.

They were well-matched dancing partners, a study in contrasts and similarities. The family resemblance was undeniable. Charlie noted that Brigitte had inherited from her father the charming, crooked smile he found so mesmerizing. Jean-Pierre, hair snow-white as he doffed his hat and tilted it back and forth with a flick of his wrist, moved with the grace of a natural athlete but, in deference to his age, with no excess motion. Brigitte, her ponytail dark and sleek, held her energy in check, matching the pace set by her father as they danced in tandem.

When they broke into simultaneous but separate routines, she took the more demanding maneuvers, shuffling in a wide circle around her father while he swayed and rocked his cane to the beat of the kazoo music. Then, graciously, with obvious respect for the man with whom she shared the floor, Brigitte stepped out of the spotlight while her father danced a solo, executing a clever combination of steps he must have been performing for audiences since before she was born.

Charlie watched her move into the shadows, appreciating the details of her silhouette: the flared hem of her skirt, the high-heeled shoes, the shapely calves, the slender ankles. He was studying her so intently that it came as a surprise to him when she suddenly stretched her arm out to meet her father's as he guided her back into the light to finish their dance.

They ended the dance with Jean-Pierre kneeling on one knee and Brigitte perched on the other. It was easy to see why they were favorites with the Dumont regulars, for their mutual affection was obvious. Jean-Pierre pretended to almost fall and dump Brigitte on her backside. Catching her balance, Brigitte giggled, toppled the hat from his head and mussed his hair. Jean-Pierre flipped her hat away and gave her ponytail a playful yank, and the audience responded with affectionate applause.

Charlie battled with his resentment. Being the center of attention came so easily to Brigitte Dumont! She knew instinctively how to play to a crowd, adapting her act as effortlessly and intuitively as a chameleon changing colors after leaping from leaves onto soil. Charlie resented the sincerity of the attention she paid her father, tasted the bitterness of knowing that he had been little more than an accessory when Brigitte had plunged her fingers through *his* hair.

*All those years*, he thought morosely. *All those years spent at the drawing board, trying to find the right com-*

*bination of image and story. He'd finally discovered it; but
what had it gotten him?* He was wealthy now, a celebrity.
His name and success were being used as a drawing card
for BARF's fund-raiser. As a result, he was a special guest
at the Chalet Dumont. He'd been personally greeted by a
Dumont and given a corner suite with a view. He'd been
interviewed and photographed and marched onto the
stage like a trained bear in a second-rate traveling circus.
But he'd kissed Brigitte Dumont. He'd tasted her sweetness, held her in his arms.

The sudden realization that he was little more than a
stage prop to her hurt his ego—and his heart.

# 4

THE FANTASY FUZZ CAKE with its femme-fatale-festooned petits fours was wheeled in by a team of waiters before Brigitte and her father had straightened from their last bow. Brigitte called Gérard out for the appropriate accolades, then gratefully abandoned the stage for the relative serenity of the family table.

Digging her fork into a slice of the cake, taking perverse pleasure in decapitating one of Gérard's icing ladies in the process, she asked, "So, where's the subject of this evening's mirth, anyway?"

"He bolted while you and Père were taking your bows," Stephen replied.

"He was mobbed for autographs after leaving the stage.... Do you think he might be angry?" her father asked, concerned.

"I don't think so," Stephen said.

"Maybe Donna talked him into a very private interview," Brigitte suggested, not liking the prospect. She'd noticed that Donna was missing, as well as Battle.

"No. She left in the middle of the sing-along," Stephen reported. "She said something about getting started on her article."

If a reporter were planning a tryst with a celebrity subject, wouldn't she be a little more original in her excuses for cutting out early? Brigitte certainly hoped so, although she was at a loss to understand why it should matter to her in the least if Mr. C. H. Battle and Donna wanted to sneak off together and play Babycakes games. "Gérard was proud of his little-women on the baby cakes. He'll be devastated if he finds out C. H. Battle never even saw it," she said.

"Maybe Mr. Battle *should* see it," Stephen replied. Then, noting Brigitte's suspicious lift of an eyebrow, he added, "For the sake of Gérard's ego."

"We can't chain our guests to their chairs and make them stay for dessert," Brigitte said quickly, grasping the general direction Stephen was headed and wanting to put him off.

"The cake was made in his honor, Brigitte. It only seems hospitable that someone should take him a piece."

"Stephen's idea is not a bad one," her father interjected, his native French accent heavier than usual—a dead giveaway that he was working at being charming. "I do not like that our special guest left early. He may have been upset by the autograph seekers, or he might be ill. If you took him a piece of the cake, you could make sure that all is well with him."

"Why me?" Brigitte asked, realizing that everyone at the table was looking at her. "How did I get elected?"

"Hospitality," Stephen explained. "It's your job, isn't it?"

"The maid was instructed to turn down his bed and leave a chocolate. Do we have to personally tuck the covers under his chin?"

"Whatever it takes," Stephen said with a shrug.

"Thank you, big brother," Brigitte told him. "It's so nice to know you're looking out for my virtue."

"Your virtue would hardly be compromised by a simple piece of cake, Brigitte," her father said.

"Oh, for . . ." Brigitte began, then gave in. "All right. I'll take the man a piece of cake. You wouldn't happen to know whether he prefers blondes, redheads or brunettes? Gérard made all three. As long as I'm going to pander to C. H. Battle's every whim, why not fulfill his fantasies?"

"See if they have any brunettes with ponytails," Stephen said dryly. "He couldn't keep his eyes off you while you were dancing."

"Give me a break!" Brigitte grumbled.

Stephen looked at their father and grinned. "Do you think it's love?"

"The lady doth protest too much," he agreed.

"The things I put up with!" Brigitte said, rising. "If I don't show up for breakfast, send in the Mounties!"

"If you don't show up for breakfast, I'll send a tray for two to Mr. Battle's room," her father teased.

Brigitte rolled her eyes in exasperation. "Père!"

"Take the man his cake, Brigitte."

"Just keep one foot flat on the floor at all times," Stephen advised.

Brigitte ignored the last gibe. Minutes later, cake plate in hand, she set out for C. H. Battle's suite, praying all the way that she didn't interrupt a tête-à-tête between *Fantasy Fuzz*'s creator and *Contemporary Canada*'s star reporter.

In defiance of the butterflies flapping their wings in her stomach, she knocked firmly, telling herself it was embarrassment she feared rather than the idea of finding Battle entertaining another woman just hours after he'd kissed her with such gusto. The knob jiggled immediately, which she took as a hopeful sign that he couldn't have been *too* involved in a passionate encounter.

He opened the door an inch or so and peeped out—not so positive a sign—then, recognizing Brigitte, stepped back to allow her inside. "Hi."

Was she just imagining his delight as he greeted her? She *wasn't* imagining the relief she felt when there was no evidence of a guest in his suite. She held out the dessert plate. "The pastry chef prepared a special Fantasy Fuzz cake with petits fours with women on them—his version of Babycakes. I . . . we . . . thought you might want to see it."

"It's . . . clever," he said, studying the icing art with interest.

"I'll pass along your comment to the chef."

"Please. Do that. He obviously went to a lot of trouble."

"He's a *Fantasy Fuzz* fan. He left a copy of this week's comics at the desk. If you'd autograph it tomorrow when you check out, he'd be thrilled."

"I'll do that."

They fell silent for a moment. Battle's shirt was untucked, the wrinkled shirttails dangling over his pants, and he'd taken off his shoes and was padding about in his socks. They were alone, standing close enough to each other for Brigitte to smell his cologne. The intimacy suddenly made her self-conscious.

"Do you mind signing autographs all the time?" she asked.

He hesitated before answering, as though he wasn't sure himself how he felt about it. "Not really. I mean, it's nice to have fans. If it weren't for them . . ."

He left the sentence dangling, leaving Brigitte wondering exactly how he would have finished it if he was totally honest. He seemed to appreciate having readers, but didn't seem entirely comfortable being the center of attention.

"You left the dining room rather quickly," she said.

He shrugged. "I thought I was finished."

"My father thought you might have been upset by the autograph seekers."

Another stretch of dead silence followed, during which Battle gave her face a thorough appraisal that made her uncomfortable. "Is that why you're here?" he asked, his voice brusque enough to make the question sound like an accusation.

"It's part of the reason," she replied evenly. "We wanted to make sure you were comfortable."

*We. The Chalet Dumont imperial "we."* That single word triggered a profound disappointment in Charlie. For a few minutes he'd been foolish enough to hope the visit might be personal—instead, it was just another variation of the "Chalet Dumont Pampers C. H. Battle" theme.

Still another awkward silence. "*Are* you comfortable?" Brigitte asked, striving but not quite succeeding in keeping the taint of sarcasm from her inquiry.

"There's nothing wrong with me that a little exercise wouldn't fix."

"Exercise?" He certainly had the ability to surprise her.

He rolled his shoulders like a woolly bear scratching against a tree trunk. "I feel a little tight. Public appearances..." He grinned self-consciously—a little-boy grin guaranteed to melt the heart of females of any age. "I was going to go down to your fitness room until I saw in the brochure that it closes early on Mondays for Family Night."

Brigitte gave him a feminine version of his grin. "We'll stoop to anything to fill the dining room." She paused. "You know, Mr. Battle—"

"Charlie."

"Charlie. You're a man of influence. You know people in positions of power. If you really wanted to work out—"

"I wouldn't want to be any trouble."

"Nonsense! We close the spa one night a week so Housekeeping can give it a good cleaning, but they probably finished an hour ago."

"I dunno...."

"Aw, come on, Charlie." She gave him a gentle tap on the midriff with the back of her hand. "I'll do some aerobics while you tread or curl or whatever."

Charlie scratched the back of his neck contemplatively. "I'd have to change clothes—"

"The bathroom door has a lock," Brigitte said.

"If you really don't mind—"

"What do you want, Charlie? That I should put it in writing?" she demanded, with a Bronx-mother affectation.

Minutes later, he emerged from the bathroom wearing a muscle shirt and fleece warm-up pants. Not wanting to embarrass him, Brigitte stifled the impulse to whistle and compliment him on his substantial pecs.

"You must lift weights," she said in the elevator, trying to thwart another extended silence.

"I like to stay in shape." *Step right up, folks. See the amazing transformation of a teenage wimp into a reasonably fit adult male.*

"What'll it be—cross-country skiing or jogging treadmill?" Brigitte asked once they were in the spa.

"I've been wanting to try a cross-country machine."

"An excellent choice, for ze whole-body workout, *monsieur!*" she teased. She helped him mount the skis and pointed out the speed controls. "I'm going to get into my gear and do some aerobics. I'll be right in that room if you need anything." She indicated a glass enclosure with mirrors lining the interior wall.

Already into the rhythm of the machine, Charlie nodded as she walked away.

"Yo!" she called, a few minutes later as she stepped out of the locker room wearing a tank top, jogging shorts, aerobics shoes and sports anklets, all of which matched. Charlie lifted a hand from the pole to return her wave and bobbed his chin in greeting. He was beginning to feel the exertion of the exercise, but hadn't yet broken into a sweat. *That* was subject to change, he reflected, as he watched her moving around inside the glass cubicle in those skimpy shorts. He was warming up rapidly—but not from the skiing.

She put a videocassette into a player connected to a television screen mounted on brackets extending from the mirrored wall. From the cross-country machine, Charlie had a clear view of the aerobics instructor on the screen and a full-length view of Brigitte's back. Brigitte's back. The ponytail that bounced when she moved. Her narrow shoulders and slender arms. Her upper back above the neck of the tank top. Her shapely legs. Her derriere—

Charlie swallowed to moisten his dry throat. He'd noticed her backside, of course. The feminine fullness, the slight sway of her hips as she walked. But he hadn't fully realized...hadn't anticipated...hadn't fully *appreciated* exactly how delectable that bottom would be in a clinging pair of shorts.

She moved along with the instructor on the screen— reaching, stretching, twisting, bending—and Charlie devoured her every movement with his eyes—wanting, wishing, yearning, desiring. Remembering the way her body had warmed as he held her in his arms. Remembering the way her lips had molded to his. Remembering the sheen of passion in her eyes as she looked at him when he'd released her. Remembering the reassuring squeezes she'd given his arm as they stood on the stage.

The videotaped aerobics instructor began to dance. Brigitte danced. The more complicated the dance theme, the more flamboyant Brigitte's movements became; and the more flamboyant Brigitte's movements became, the less attention Charlie paid to cross-country skiing. He lost his timing and nearly stumbled off the machine. Cursing under his breath, he righted himself, and resolved to stare straight ahead instead of into the glass-walled room.

His resolve lasted six seconds. A slender tenth of a minute later his gaze was once again solidly fixed on Brigitte Dumont's backside. She was doing some kind of kicks, and when she raised her leg, the pants stretched taut against the fullness of her buttocks and rode up to afford him teasing glances at the crease where thigh and buttocks met.

He lost his timing and stumbled again after Brigitte executed a particularly high kick. Finally he turned off the machine and stepped down from the imitation skis. He went over to the glass enclosure, where he stood in the doorway and watched Brigitte dance.

Catching sight of him, she stopped in midstep, her shoulders sagging dramatically, as though she might collapse from the exertion of the exercise. "Problem?"

"Just watching." After a beat, he added, "That looks complicated."

"It's just a few basic steps and some kicks. Want to give it a try?"

Charlie looked near panic as he shook his head. "I, uh, don't dance."

"Ever?"

She made it sound as radical as not being able to use knives and forks, indoor plumbing facilities or remote controls for television. Charlie shrugged off the implied censure. "I never learned."

Brigitte walked to the video player and turned off the tape. "Really?"

"We can't all be Dumonts."

He sounded offended, and Brigitte said quickly, "I didn't mean there was anything . . . I've just never known anyone who didn't know how to dance."

A dreadful silence followed. Eventually Charlie asked, "How long have you been dancing with your father like you did tonight?"

Brigitte hit the rewind button on the video player. "The soft-shoe routines? I can't remember when I didn't know them. Père taught Claire when she was old enough to learn the steps, and I just sort of absorbed the routines from watching them. The three of us danced together for a while, then Claire bowed out of the act the first time she got pregnant."

"What about your brother?"

"Stephen? He knows all the routines, but he's not too keen on performing. We've been teaching Janet the 'Tea for Two' steps, but the kazoo chorus is her thing."

The video player switched off with a popping sound. Brigitte took the tape out and put it back into its place on the shelf. She turned back to Charlie. "So, why didn't you ever learn to dance?"

She sounded more interested than critical, and Charlie no longer felt defensive. "Two left feet?"

"I can't believe that," Brigitte responded with a sly smile. "You ski, don't you? And lift weights. Surely you could master a simple box step."

"What's a box step?" Charlie asked.

"I could show you," she offered brightly.

Embarrassed, Charlie hedged. "I probably wouldn't—"

"Of course, you would. It wouldn't take ten minutes. Let me see if I can find something easy to dance to. We keep a lot of tapes here for aerobics. There has to be something suitable."

He started to protest again, but she was reading labels on the cassettes with a determined expression. "This ought to do," she murmured, inserting a tape into the stereo system.

The music was slow and mellow, and Charlie knew he was in trouble. He was going to have to touch her again, and when he was touching her he was going to remember how little clothing she was wearing, instead of focusing on the fact that she was only doing her duty as hostess to a Chalet Dumont celebrity guest.

She stepped in front of him and stood there looking up at him expectantly. Unsure what he was supposed to do, Charlie shifted his weight from one foot to the other. She smiled at him—not mockingly, but gently—and lifted her right arm away from her body. "We might as well do this properly. Your left hand, please."

He raised his arm awkwardly. Brigitte cupped his hand in hers, turning it gently. "Palm up, please. And I put my palm over yours, and you curl your fingers around mine, firmly, but not too... That's good. And this—" she placed her left hand lightly on his shoulder "—goes here, so I can feel any subtle movement of your shoulder."

She smiled up at him. "It'll help me anticipate your footwork."

Charlie smiled back at her, grateful that he didn't have to say anything at the moment, since there was a lump in his throat the size of a small country. From his point of view, the question of whether she could anticipate his footwork by feeling any subtle movements of his shoulder paled in comparison to the fact that the side of her hand had landed on bare skin.

Brigitte tilted her head toward his right arm. "Your arm goes around me, and your hand should rest just under my shoulder blade."

Was he imagining the slightly breathless quality in her voice when she said, "Officially, this is the standard dance position. Of course, there are variations."

"Variations?" he asked, lost in the dreamy expression of her eyes.

"Some—" She swallowed. "Sometimes couples dance a little closer together, or a man holds the woman's hand against his chest, or the woman's arm goes around his neck."

"Oh."

"A lot depends on...how tall they are in relation to each other...."

"How tall?"

"Uh-hmm." It was almost a musical reply. The song she'd chosen was lulling, seductive. "Or what kind of music, or how much..."

"How much?" he prompted after she let the statement hang unfinished for a minor eternity, while that dreamy quality in her eyes grew more pronounced.

"How much they enjoy dancing together," she said, in a cross between a whisper and a sigh.

She seemed to have been getting more and more relaxed—her hand was growing heavier on his shoulder. Now she dropped her gaze to stare at his chest, and he felt her body tense as she sucked in a deep breath. "We might as well start with the standard procedure," she told him. "There'll be plenty of time for variations once you get the steps down."

Brigitte lifted her gaze to his face again, and he was disappointed to see that the dreaminess had disappeared. She was all business now, friendly but not involved as she looked down at their feet. "You're going to have to be patient with me. I'm going to be telling you to do just the opposite of what I'm doing, and it's going to take some concentration. Let's see, I'm stepping back with my right foot, so you step forward with your left. Good. Now, forward and sideways with the right. Uh-hmm. Now, move your left foot next to your right and shift your weight to it."

She looked up at him. "That wasn't so tough, was it?"

Charlie shook his head.

"Then, relax a little. All we have to do now is get back to where we started. Essentially, you just reverse your movements. Straight back with the right. Uh-hmm. Good. Now, back and to the side with the left. Now, close the gap, and you're home."

She flashed him an approving smile. "That's the box step. All you have to do is repeat it over and over."

Charlie chuckled in delight. "That's all there is to it?"

"Well, it's not the lambada, or the tango. But the box step'll get you through most dance situations. Once you get familiar enough with it, you can embellish a bit. Try it again, in time with the music."

"Left foot forward," Charlie said as he took the step. "Then right foot, then—"

"Together," she prompted, when he hesitated. "And shift weight, then back."

Charlie's movements were slightly wooden, but he completed the step without further prompting, and they danced together through several repetitions with few missteps. Gradually he became more confident in his movements, and Brigitte yielded the lead, following him smoothly.

"You're a fast learner," Brigitte said.

"I didn't know dancing would be this easy." *Or this wonderful.* How was he going to let her go when the music stopped?

"Why didn't you ever learn?"

"I guess I never had anyone to teach me."

Their bodies gravitated together. Brigitte's hand was now splayed over his nape, her fingertips touching his hairline. "You've got a lot of time to catch up on," she told him, tucking her cheek against his chest.

The top of her head just fit under his chin, and Charlie found her hair soft against his skin, the scent of it alluring. "Ummm," he agreed. *I'd like to do all my catching up right now, right here, tonight, with you, holding you like this.*

It would be enough, he thought. A night spent holding her would make up for all the girls that gangly teenager he'd been had never danced with; for all the dances he'd never gone to because he was too shy to ask a girl out; for the deprivation of a boy who'd yearned but had lacked the confidence to reach. *It would be enough—if she were with him because she wanted to be with him, and not just because he was a celebrity guest of the Chalet Dumont.*

Brigitte sighed contentedly against Charlie's chest. She couldn't remember when it had felt this good being in a man's arms. Folded against his strength, she felt nurtured by it. The chest beneath her cheek was wide and firm; the arm wrapped around her, strong and hard; and the hand wrapped around hers, powerful but gentle. The fleece warm-up pants Charlie wore accentuated the natural warmth of a fit male body. The fabric was soft against her skin as their thighs brushed, but beneath the surface softness, there was the contrast of powerful muscle. It was an odd sensation—that combination of softness and hardness pressing against her bare skin—but nice; at the same time both comforting and stimulating.

The intimacy of the way he held her left no doubt that he found her desirable. She found him desirable, as well, and fantasized about what kind of lover he would be. Such a strong man. So much power in those hard muscles. A shiver slid up her spine as she imagined what it would be like to have that power unleashed in the physical act of sexual expression. Even tempered with kindness and gentleness, it would be spectacular. *He* would be spectacular.

Memories of their kiss set her senses tingling. She recalled it in detail—the way he'd pulled her ponytail back, the expression of near savage yearning in his eyes as he lowered his face to hers, the intensity that communicated itself in the way he'd drawn her against him. There had been such urgency, such ardor. When he'd released her, they both had been stunned by the power of the attraction between them, and by the sense of something having started.

*Until he'd turned away to call Donna "Babycakes."*

Brigitte opened her eyes to the sight of their hands, fingers entwined, resting on his chest next to her cheek. Had he moved them, or had she? It mattered not who, only that they'd instinctively moved together.

*And if she didn't do something very soon, she was going to be Babycakes Number One Thousand Fifty-Nine or so.*

Yet she was loath to move away from him. The chemistry between them was hypnotizing; it made the idea of moving away seem absurd. It made her want to believe that anything so special to her, *must* be special to him, as well.

Common sense, logic, some lingering instinct for self-preservation nagged at her through that illogical dance of sensual persuasion, reminding her that Babycakes Number One through One Thousand Fifty-Eight probably had felt the same way. What his lumbering bashful-schoolboy routine, yearning glances and bulging muscles did for her, they had surely done for other women. Just because his effect on her was extraordinary, she had no reason to believe her effect on him was unusual to him. Of course, there was the imposing evidence that he found her attractive—

Brigitte stopped dancing. Ceasing all movement, she stood rigid as a statue. Charlie very nearly tripped over his own feet to keep from stepping on hers. "Brigitte?"

She didn't answer him.

"What's wrong?"

Brigitte took a step back, putting space between them. A safety margin. A collect-your-wits-to-survive margin.

"You stopped dancing," Charlie said, as though he felt the need to justify his concern.

"I was just . . . wondering."

He refused to tolerate half an answer. "What?"

"Whether you could kiss a woman and mean it."

# 5

CHARLIE'S SURPRISE was evident. "You were thinking about kissing me?"

"Yes!" Brigitte admitted begrudgingly. Her shoulders drooped as she sighed forlornly. "Unfortunately."

Charlie crossed his arms over his waist. Brigitte bit the inside of her lip to keep from grinning as she noted irreverently that in that stance, and in his muscle shirt, he looked a little like Mr. Clean with hair and no earring.

He glowered at her a moment, then hurled the question at her with the concentration of a shot-putter putting shot: "What's that supposed to mean?"

"It means that I find you attractive. And you make me feel . . . sexy and desirable."

A horrible possibility crossed Charlie's mind. "You're not married, are you?" *Women got married and kept their maiden names, didn't they?*

"Married?"

"Or engaged or involved or anything?"

"Do you think I'd be here alone with you, dancing, if I were?"

"If you're not married or engaged or anything, then why don't you want to think about kissing me?"

"Because I'm afraid to take you seriously."

"Why?" Charlie bellowed.

"Because you don't take women seriously."

Charlie recognized the injustice when it slapped him in the face. Of all the men in the world, he was surely in the top one percent when it came to taking women seriously.

If *anyone* took women seriously, it was Charles H. Battle. No one could be as terrified of, mystified by, or in awe of *anything* as Charlie Battle was of women. He took women seriously the way he took earthquakes, avalanches and agitated bears seriously. The way he took the escalating crime rate, rising cost of living and environmental plundering seriously. The way he took difficult ski slopes seriously. The way he took chocolate-swirl ice cream seriously.

"What the hell do you mean, I don't take women seriously?"

"You call them Babycakes!"

Charlie's mouth dropped open in consternation, and snapped shut a second later. "Baby—? *Fantasy Fuzz* calls women Babycakes, not Charlie Battle."

"You called *me* Babycakes."

"You're playing the part!"

"You called Donna Babycakes."

"Donna who?"

"The reporter!" Brigitte snapped, with a little thrill that he'd had to ask.

Charlie plunged a hand into his hair. "It was what Fantasy Fuzz would have said. I was embarrassed."

"Embarrassed?"

"Weren't you?"

"Of course, but—"

"I didn't know what to say, so I said what Fantasy would have said under the same circumstances."

"I wasn't sure you were serious about the kiss."

"You're kidding, eh?" If he'd been any more serious, the reporter would have been the one embarrassed!

"I wasn't sure you were kissing *me*."

"Who the hell did you think I was kissing?"

Brigitte answered lamely, "Babycakes."

"That's just plain dumb!"

"I thought you were just taking advantage of the situation."

"Is that a fact?"

The cutting edge of sarcasm in his voice would have been intimidating even if he weren't as physically imposing as a mountain. Brigitte was contemplating how to defuse his anger when he took a step toward her.

"I had as much cause to think *you* were taking advantage of the situation as you had to think I was."

Her eyes widened as she stared into his. "What?"

"You. The way you turn it on and off."

Brigitte had the vague sense of being insulted. "Turn *what* on and off?"

"The hospitality. The charm. The...whatever that was you did in the dining room, rubbing up against me and running your fingers through my hair."

"That was . . . publicity for the mystery weekend."

"So was kissing for the photographer."

"Is that all it was for you?"

"Is that all it was for you?"

"That depends," Brigitte said broodingly.

"On what?"

"On whether it meant something to you," she told him. "On whether you were aware that you were kissing a woman named Brigitte, and not just the most convenient, available female body who answers to 'Babycakes.'"

"It meant something," he reassured gravely.

A prolonged, tension-filled silence followed, during which Charlie reflected on exactly how much that kiss had meant. Too much for safety. Brigitte's eyes held both vulnerability and challenge as she looked up at him, and Charlie wanted her so desperately at that moment that the intensity of his desire for her frightened him. He was terrified of touching her for fear he wouldn't be able to let her go; yet, if he didn't touch her—

"You want to know if I can kiss a woman and mean it?"
It was as much an indictment as a question, but he left her
no opportunity to answer before pulling her into his arms.

There was no gentleness at first, only a determined intensity that stole Brigitte's breath away as his mouth fused
with hers. Then she slid her arms around his neck and
parted her lips, encouraging Charlie to deepen the kiss.

Charlie kissed her because she was beautiful and spirited and he'd never met anyone who intrigued him more.
She kissed him back because he was virile and a little
bashful and a little dangerous and utterly fascinating. Instinctively, he drew her closer, lifting her to him. Brigitte
was scarcely aware of her feet leaving the ground. *Such a
kiss from such a man.*

The kiss went on and on, until she knew it could no
longer remain a kiss without becoming something more.
There was sweetness in the way he lowered her until her
feet touched the floor and eased away from her, until there
was perhaps a quarter inch of space between them.

Brigitte opened her eyes to find his face near hers, his
gaze appreciative, adoring. She wanted to smile, but it was
too soon. She wanted to say something, but nothing appropriate or adequate sprang to mind. So she just looked
up at him, telling him without words of the pleasure he'd
given her, of the magic his touch worked on her, of the way
she wished the kiss could have gone on forever without
having either to end or to grow into something more, and
that maybe, when she knew him better, it wouldn't have
to end.

Emotionally, sensually, Charlie had consumed more
than his fill. He ached, but it was a good ache, like having
muscles too tight after a taxing session on the weight
bench. But full as he was, full to overflowing, he felt even
more when he looked at Brigitte's face. Her lips were puffy
from the pressure of his mouth. A blush of sexual excitement reddened her cheeks flatteringly. For the duration of

a kiss, she had given herself to him, let herself be vulnerable to him. And as she looked up at him trustingly, her eyes told him that she was as moved by the experience as he, that she could do it again, that the same yearning that consumed him consumed her, as well.

"I meant that," he whispered hoarsely, wishing the words didn't sound so harsh.

She raised her hand to his face and trailed her fingertip lightly over his cheek. His words had been a whisper.

"I believe you did."

A mellow silence followed. They savored the gradual return to reality from their venture into sensual lunacy.

Brigitte knew that eventually one of them had to speak, to break the spell, and she reverted to her role as hostess. "Do you want to try any of the other equipment?"

After a beat, they both laughed at the absurdity of the phrasing of her question. "It's time I went back to my room." Charlie cocked his head and grinned.

Brigitte looked down at her shorts and tank top. "I've got to change clothes. Do you think you can find your room okay?"

"Sure." He bobbed his head toward the ski machine. "Thanks for—"

"My pleasure."

He seemed reluctant to move, but finally took several steps toward the door before stopping. Turning, he met her gaze. She looked at him expectantly.

He appeared almost tormented. "If you ever look at me again the way you looked at me after . . . I won't be able to let go of you again, Brigitte."

Brigitte nodded acknowledgement.

Charlie headed for the door again with the haste of a man who'd just shed a heavy burden and was anxious to be on his way.

"Charlie." Brigitte spoke softly, barely above a whisper, but her entreaty stopped him in midstep. He turned

to look at her, and she saw reflected in his eyes all the hope
and fear-tinged doubt she was feeling.

"If I ever look at you like that again, you won't have to
let go."

For a tense moment she wondered if he were going to sail
across the room and sling her over his shoulders and carry
her off. Her mind wasn't working well enough to wonder
where he might take her. Such practicalities were inconsequential as her scalp prickled in response to the gleam
of naked desire in his eyes, and her breath stuck in her
throat. The force drawing them together was too elemen-
tal for logic, too strong for denial.

She stood there, holding her breath, and waited for him
to make the next move. He opened his mouth as if to speak
but snapped it shut, as though afraid of what he might say,
then fled the room.

Brigitte sighed as she stared at the door that closed behind him. "Next time, Charlie," she said aloud, and then
whispered, "Next time, you won't have to let go."

"YOU'LL NEVER BELIEVE the profile that's emerging of C. H.
Battle," Donna said. "I've been chasing down people who
knew him 'when' for two days."

Brigitte frowned into the telephone receiver. "I thought
you were doing a story on the BARF mystery weekend."

"That's just a sidebar, the local angle. C. H. Battle is the
real story. I thought you might have a choice bit of information to add."

"Me? I just met the man two hours before you did."

"Don't be coy, Brigitte. I saw that kiss, remember?"
Donna said, suggestively.

*But not the next one, thank goodness!* Brigitte thought.
Glad Donna couldn't see the idiotic smile that had settled
on her face, she tried to sound noncommittal. "Oh, that.
That was just a publicity shot."

"That kiss was at least a seven on the Richter scale."

"Well," Brigitte admitted mischievously.

"I knew it!" Donna exclaimed. "What a hunk! And you'll never believe... Until *Fantasy Fuzz* made him famous, the man was a total recluse. Practically a hermit."

"That explains it," Brigitte said under her breath.

Trust Donna to have supersonic hearing. "Explains what?"

"Nothing," Brigitte replied.

"Uh-uh, Brigitte. You're not getting away with that. *What* does Battle's being a hermit explain?"

Brigitte scowled at the receiver, knowing that if she hedged on telling Donna what she'd been thinking, Donna would nag it out of her. The woman was as tenacious as a pit bull when she got her teeth into a story. It probably made her a good reporter, but sometimes it made her an irritating friend.

"He didn't know how to dance," Brigitte said reluctantly.

"You *danced* with him?"

"Not— We were in the workout room and I was doing aerobics, and he said he'd never learned to dance so I showed him a box step. End of story." *End of one story, beginning of another....*

Smiling again, she traced the lines of the cartoon that had been propped on her desk since the previous afternoon when she'd found it in her message box. Drawn on Chalet Dumont stationery, it showed a man and a woman wearing workout clothes dancing together. The characters, though cartoon characters, bore a more-than-coincidental resemblance to Charlie Battle and Brigitte Dumont. Instead of C. H. Battle, he'd signed the cartoon "Charlie," and above the signature, he'd written, "Thanks for a meaningful experience."

"Why don't I believe that?"

"Believe what?" Brigitte asked. She'd forgotten Donna was on the other end of the line.

"That the private dancing lessons you just told me about were simply a serendipitous happenstance."

"Heavens!" Brigitte teased, trying to sidetrack her friend. "A serendipitous happenstance? I'm not that kind of woman."

"I didn't think so. But, obviously, you're not going to tell all. The photos are great, by the way. Do you want a couple of prints for a marquee?"

Brigitte said she did, and Donna promised to mail them. They arrived two days later. As reported, they were excellent photos—so excellent that Brigitte's father commented that he hadn't realized C. H. Battle would be quite so grateful to get a piece of cake. Brigitte refrained from trying to point out that the photo was taken before the cake was even wheeled into the dining room.

Stephen was so impressed that he started calling Brigitte "Babycakes" as though she'd never had any other name. Nicole and Jennifer followed their beloved uncle's example, despite their amused mother's halfhearted admonitions not to do so. Brigitte secretly suspected that Claire welcomed their preoccupation with calling their aunt silly names, since it somewhat supplanted Nicole's preoccupation with French bras.

Claude, being Claude, merely grinned whenever the photo was mentioned, and Brigitte's mother remarked more than once on the nobility of Brigitte's dedication to environmental issues.

Brigitte endured their teasing with stoicism worthy of a Dumont, smug in the knowledge that none of her tormentors knew the extent of her interest in C. H. Battle. *They* didn't know how often she thought about that kiss...and the other one. They didn't know how often she thought of Charlie—she could think of him no other way now—or how vivid the memories of their time alone were to her. They had not spied the cartoon on her desk, nor read the revealing note scribbled in the corner, nor caught her touching that page of Chalet Dumont stationery and smiling. Her attraction to Charlie Battle remained her secret. It was still too private to share, too precarious for the scrutiny of others. She felt protective of it.

Brigitte had been flirting with men ever since she'd discovered there was a difference between the sexes, and the Chalet Dumont had obligingly provided an endless line of men on whom to perfect the ancient rite of courtship. Vast experience over time had given her a rare perspective on the mystical forces that drew two people together, and it would have been futile for her to try to deny to herself that there was something extraordinary about the attraction she felt for Charlie Battle.

She hadn't the faintest idea what set him apart from any of the other men that had paraded in and out of the chalet. He was not the best-looking man she'd ever met. His face was more interesting than handsome. And it wasn't as though she had never seen muscles; the chalet was practically wall-to-wall ski sweaters during the season— most of them covering impressive male chests. Nor had he bowled her over with his charming personality. He was polite, but hardly jovial or expansive. Of course, there was that meltdown thing he did with his eyes, which brought a warm flush to her cheeks each time she remembered it—

No. Brigitte didn't know what set Charlie Battle apart from the other men she'd met. She just knew that while the rest of the family awaited C. H. Battle's return with curiosity about what roles he'd cast them in in the murder mystery, she looked forward to finding out if, on second meeting, Charlie Battle remained a man apart from other men.

In the interim, she monitored the reservations made for the BARF event daily. Four couples had signed up following the Family Night preview, and reservations had trickled in at the rate of one or two couples per day since. Two weeks before the cutoff, the count stood at less than half capacity. Brigitte knew that the bulk of the reservations came in on the last few days before any cutoff date, but she found herself having to reassure some of the other BARF committee members who were less familiar with the industry that the number of early reservations was a strong indicator that the event would be a sellout.

Her job provided plenty of diversion from her preoccupation with Death at the Dumont. On one particularly harrowing day, she dealt with a bride and groom who kept changing their minds about details for their wedding reception, a committee of class-reunion organizers who couldn't agree on anything about their dinner dance, a lost shipment of kazoos and numerous other indecisive customers and minor crises intrinsic to her job.

The incoming mail provided the one spot of brightness on that wretched day. The return address alone, scrawled in Charlie's script, lifted her spirits. Inside were two sheets of Charlie's letterhead. The first instructed Brigitte to tell the sculptor making the body for the mystery weekend to simulate facial bruises and a bullet hole in the chest.

He'd divided the second page into five panels, the first four of which were filled with two sets of footprints, one distinctively male, the other female. Brigitte grinned as she realized the phantom feet were executing a perfect box step, but it was the final panel that turned a grin into a full-fledged smile. Instead of footprints, it was filled with an exaggerated exclamation point surrounded by exploding firecrackers and soaring rockets—a cartoon sketch of a kiss.

Brigitte was still smiling as she lifted the receiver to call the sculptor. She read Charlie's message about the victim's body to the woman, then dropped the body note in the file folder she'd labeled Death At The Dumont. The new cartoon remained on her desk next to the sketch Charlie had titled *A Meaningful Experience.*

A few days later, photocopied page proofs of the *Contemporary Canada* article arrived. Donna hadn't exaggerated. Charles H. Battle's life story made fascinating reading. His father, a Chicago Police Department homicide detective, had been killed in a shoot-out during which he'd saved the life of a fellow police officer. For his valor under fire, he'd been awarded a medal of merit posthumously. Charlie had been fourteen at the time.

Charlie's mother, Canadian by birth, had moved back to Alberta to be near her aging parents. Charlie hadn't adapted well to the change of country and life-style. Quiet and shy, he'd been a mediocre student in high school. Fellow classmates recalled that he kept to himself outside the classroom, and his only record of involvement in school activities was in the school's annual art competitions.

"He was always doodling in his notebook while the rest of us were taking notes. We considered him a little spooky," a former classmate remarked.

"In college," Donna wrote, "he remained something of a recluse in the general student community, although he became part of a tight-knit group of art majors."

"We were awed by his talent and his focus," one of his fellow student artists recalled. "He was never into partying or anything like the rest of us. He just loved art, the process of creation."

"What had been perceived as spookiness in high school now had evolved into charisma," Donna's narrative continued. She backed up her statement with another quote from a female art student who had been an acquaintance of Charlie's.

"He was the strong, silent type," she recalled. "It gave him an air of mystery. We all wished he would ask us out, but he never did. We could never figure out why. It was obvious he was interested in girls. He had a way of looking at you—"

*So* he'd perfected "the look" long before he met her. Frowning, she read on. "He was equally as reclusive while employed at the advertising firm of Kilman and Kilman."

"His work was always right on target," said a co-worker. "It had a very distinctive style. But aside from the work, he was rather detached. He was there, but he wasn't *there*. He'd made token appearances at office parties and such, but never circulated, he just . . . observed. We speculated about his private life, but none of us had a clue about it. He never mentioned the comic strips, but apparently he'd been working on them for years."

Donna concluded: "C. H. Battle is the classic overnight sensation, having worked dedicatedly for years before a hard-boiled homicide detective named Fantasy Fuzz, quite possibly based on the life of his hero father, won him critical and popular acclaim as a cartoonist. Despite his success, he remains something of a recluse, but fame has hurled him into a public spotlight. Muscular and virile . . ."

*Count on Donna to notice,* Brigitte thought with a stab of jealousy she wouldn't have admitted to.

"The confidence of success coupled with the inevitable association with his fictional creation, has imbued him with sexual charisma."

Brigitte sprang to attention when she saw her name at the beginning of the next paragraph: ". . . called upon to play Babycakes to Battle's Fantasy Fuzz in the upcoming BARF mystery weekend, termed the kiss he gave her while posing for publicity photos, 'At least a seven on the Richter scale.'"

*Words force-fed into my mouth,* Brigitte silently protested, frowning, then read on.

"Still, traces of the painfully shy young man uprooted during adolescence remain. Says Brigitte Dumont, who taught him the box step in the fitness room at the Chalet

Dumont following a recent Family Night: 'He'd never learned to dance.'"

*That wasn't for publication!* Brigitte was angry momentarily; then, sighing philosophically, tossed the tear sheets aside. At least the full-page photo of Fantasy Fuzz and Babycakes was eye-catching and the sidebar about the BARF mystery weekend made it sound like fun.

Doubtless Charlie would be clipping it for his scrapbook—it would be nourishment for any man's ego to open a magazine and discover that he's imbued with sexual charisma—especially when the article contained a testimonial that his kiss registered at least a seven on the Richter scale.

## 6

WITHIN THREE DAYS after *Contemporary Canada* hit the shelves, Death at the Dumont was fully booked, and there was a waiting list. Brigitte called the BARF president with the good news and wrote Donna an effusive thank-you note for having spread the word about the event.

It occurred to her that one other person might want to know that the weekend was a sellout. She'd been hoping—half expecting, actually—that she might hear from Charlie, but there had been nothing since the note about the body, and the cartoon.

She debated whether to call him, and decided it would be a simple courtesy to do so. In fact, she would be remiss if she didn't let him know that his generous participation in the weekend had drawn a capacity crowd. It was *imperative* that she call him. The fact that she was yearning to hear his voice was totally irrelevant.

She got to hear his voice—at least, a recording of it. It told her brusquely that he couldn't come to the phone and invited her to leave a message at the sound of the beep. She left one—crisp, friendly, direct—and invited him to call if he had any questions. She even gave him the number of her private line, so he could call her apartment instead of through the chalet's switchboard.

Apparently he had no questions. Brigitte rationalized her disappointment over not hearing from him with excuses. Perhaps he was busy. Perhaps he was out of town. Perhaps he felt there was no need to call her back since her message contained all the information she'd called to give him.

Of all the possibilities, she refused to consider that he simply no longer wished to speak to her. She couldn't believe that. Not after the tenderness of their moments together in the fitness room. Not after the way he'd kissed her. Not after seeing the cartoons he'd drawn for her and the inscription that their time together had been meaningful. Not when she was counting the days until he returned to the Chalet Dumont, and was waiting to resume where they'd left off in the fitness room.

And then it occurred to her: The answering machine might have malfunctioned. He might not have heard the message at all. Perhaps she could call him again to make sure—

As quickly as hope flared, common sense prevailed. The machine seemed to have been working. The message hadn't been urgent. If she called again and he *had* gotten the message, she'd just end up feeling like a fool.

Actually, Charlie had heard her message; had, indeed, listened to it as she spoke into the speaker on the machine he'd bought to shield himself from nuisance calls that persisted even after he'd acquired an unlisted number.

Her voice had a paralyzing effect on him. He was equally powerless to pick up the receiver and talk to her or switch off the machine so that he wouldn't have to listen to her.

"Hi! This is Brigitte Dumont."

The cheer. The the-world-can-take-a-flying-leap-if-they-don't-like-it attitude. For a few seconds, he thrilled to the sound of that voice and the energy contained in it. For an instant, he remembered the pleasure of looking at her, of smelling her, of touching her. God help him, he even remembered the taste of her—a taste he craved too easily.

Then he remembered whose voice it was—the voice of Brigitte Dumont; Brigitte, the Betrayer—and he frantically scrambled to patch the gaping hole in the walls of defense he'd built around himself years earlier. She had breached his walls with her pretty face, with her crooked smile and voice that reminded him of laughter. She had put her hand in his and taught him to dance and he'd let her slip inside the walls.

She'd had him defending himself to her, assuring her of his sincerity. That must have been good for a hearty laugh. He'd been sincere—so sincere that he'd made himself vulnerable to her in a way he'd never let himself become vulnerable to a woman before. And she'd been sincere, too—sincere enough to blab about their private moments to a reporter who'd distributed that private information to all of Canada.

Yes. He'd bought the damned magazine. He was curious about what Donna had written, and he'd grinned at the photograph of himself kissing a beautiful woman, especially when that black-and-white image opened a floodgate of memories of how good the woman had felt in his arms. His ego had been boosted by the caption describing the kiss as "...At least a seven on the Richter scale." Then he'd read the second quote from Brigitte.

He didn't even remember the high-school classmate who referred to him as "spooky," so while the comment stung his pride, it didn't wound him. He was a bit dismayed that his college friend, whom he remembered fondly, would discuss him with a reporter, but what she'd said had been vaguely flattering, so he'd sloughed off that bit of treason, although the entire tone and content of the article left him feeling exposed.

It was Brigitte's betrayal that had wounded him, her indiscretion that inflicted pain. He'd let her inside the walls, and she'd attacked from within. He'd stressed to her that their time together had been meaningful, and she'd repaid him by telling the press that he'd never learned to dance. She'd asked him if he could kiss a woman and mean it, and then blithely rated their private moments the way she might score the appeal of a new song on the radio. She'd seduced him into revealing something of himself to her and then flaunted the knowledge he'd shared with her.

*He'd trusted her.* That was the core issue. He'd wanted her so badly that he'd finally allowed himself to take a chance. He might forgive her for being beautiful and spoiled and self-involved enough to trifle with the celebrity of the week, but he'd never forgive her for making him trust her and then betraying that private trust in such a public way.

In frustration, he ripped a sheet from his drawing easel, crumpled it and flung it into the trash can next to his desk with a violent gesture.

A week earlier he'd found it wryly amusing that the Babycakes character in the preliminary sketches of his new story line persistently resembled Brigitte Dumont. He'd replaced the sleek ponytail with a cap of frothy curls between the first and second drafts, straightened the smile between the second and third. Each time he'd saved the discard, planning to show them to Brigitte, imagining how he would tease her about interfering with his concentration. Or about being so impressive in the Babycakes role that she was downright inspirational.

Now those early sketches, wadded into tight balls, lined the bottom of his trash can—tangible symbols of his fury. The can was brimming full with discarded sketches.

In his mind, Charlie was certain about how he felt about Brigitte "The Betrayer" Dumont. Yet his right hand seemed to be suffering a slight case of ambivalence. Otherwise, why did it keep drawing her face?

He dreaded the upcoming weekend, but he kept the promises he made. The mystery scenario was written, the publicity was out and the event was booked to capacity.

He was a man of severe self-discipline. He could manage to play Fantasy Fuzz to Brigitte Dumont's Babycakes for a couple of days.

He only hoped he could resist the urge to insinuate an actual homicide into the tongue-in-cheek mystery. And who would blame him? Wasn't death the standard fate of traitors? And he had the perfect cover. Who would suspect the investigating homicide detective—or a world-famous cartoonist, for that matter?

Yes, homicide held a certain appeal—until he realized that homicide was too good for Brigitte Dumont. Homicide was too quick and too easy. For the divine Ms. Dumont, torture would be infinitely preferable.

BRIGITTE WAS TRYING hard not to fidget during her meeting with the class-reunion organizers. Two of the committee of five had arrived late, and every detail of the dinner dance had been hashed and rehashed, with five opinions, expressed in tedious detail on every point of negotiation.

Brigitte was tempted to offer them a boardroom for their private use and ask them to page her when they knew what they wanted, but the Chalet Dumont prided itself on its personalized service. Besides, it wasn't *their* fault their appointment fell on the afternoon Charlie Battle was scheduled to return to the chalet. So she asked guiding questions, listened to their debates, and offered suggestions when invited to do so.

By the time they'd opted for a buffet rather than a sit-down dinner, deliberated over a menu, haggled about how the tables should be arranged, and decided on a spotlighted mirrored ball over the dance floor, Brigitte was resigned to having missed her chance to greet Charlie upon his arrival. Her fears were confirmed when, after shaking the hand of the last member of the reunion committee, she caught sight of Charlie's back. Suitcase in hand, he was waiting for the elevator.

*Not fair!* she thought. She was supposed to have time to freshen up before seeing him. Now she'd be lucky to catch him. Extricating herself from the reunion committee as quickly as possible, she made a mad dash for the elevator only to see the doors slide shut before she could catch Charlie's attention. She walked to the registration desk. "Was that Mr. Battle I just saw?"

Sarah, the clerk on duty, stiffened in a telltale gesture of defense. "Yes. I explained that you'd wanted to greet him, but that your meeting was running longer than expected. I offered to call you anyway, but he said not to bother you, that he could find his room by himself."

Brigitte's sigh betrayed her disappointment. Squaring her shoulders, she said, "Well, he's a big boy. I'm sure he'll find his room all right."

"I don't think he was in a very good mood," Sarah volunteered.

*Before, or after he learned I wasn't here to greet him?* Brigitte wondered, hoping he'd been just a bit disappointed. "What makes you say that?" she asked Sarah.

"He just seemed kind of... brusque. Like he wasn't thrilled to be here."

"Hmm." Brigitte digested the information. "Did you order the gift basket?"

Sarah nodded. "As soon as he left the desk."

"Then it should be on its way up." She smiled. "I think I'll go see what else the management can do about boosting Mr. Battle's morale."

Sarah gave her a knowing I'll-bet-you-will shrug and turned to assist the guest who'd just approached the desk.

Ten minutes later, with her ponytail brushed, her bangs fluffed and a fresh application of gloss shining on her lips, Brigitte knocked on the door of Charlie's room. When he opened the door, she greeted him with an energetic hello.

Charlie made a grunting sound that apparently was supposed to pass for a reply. He remained in the doorway, as unyielding as one of the mountains outside.

Brigitte held up her right hand and twisted her wrist back and forth, showing him the stemmed crystal goblets she was holding. "I...uh...had these sitting around, and I thought you might have a bottle of wine you'd like to share."

At first he just stared at her in brooding silence. If he were a stranger she'd met in a dark alley instead of the man she'd taught to dance less than a month before, Brigitte would have been intimidated by the combination of that scowl and his size and strength.

"I don't think so," he said at last.

Not easily dissuaded, Brigitte leaned against the doorjamb provocatively and gave him a fetching smile. "I have it on good authority that you're not averse to a little nip of wine around this time in the afternoon."

"Not today."

Brigitte peeled herself from the doorjamb. "Ah, come on, Charlie. Live a little."

"I intend to do just that," Charlie assured her gravely. At the very least, he intended to survive; and self-preservation dictated that he not let himself fall under the spell of Brigitte Dumont again. Since opening the door and finding her there, radiating sexuality, he'd felt his resolve not to let her get to him crumbling faster than a soggy taco shell.

Brigitte waited for him to step aside, to do *something*, but he didn't budge. He remained in the doorway, cheerless and impenetrable as a stone gargoyle. "I've heard of getting up on the wrong side of the bed," she said. "But you act as though you didn't even see a bed last night."

*Only* Brigitte Dumont would talk to a man about beds and be that blasé. Bed was the last thing in the universe Charlie needed to discuss with Brigitte Dumont. "We're going to be going over the scenario later," he told her, gesturing at the wine bottle. "I need a clear head."

"You got the note, then, about the meeting?"

"I got it," he said, sounding as enthusiastic as a convicted murderer served with a death warrant.

Usually she could charm almost anyone out of the doldrums. But instinct—people instinct—told her this was more than a temporary pique or bad mood. Charlie wasn't just grouchy, he was hostile.

*Why?* she wanted to ask. *What happened?* But she was too stunned to pose the questions. She raised her gaze to his face, searching his eyes for some tenderness, some sign that he remembered those magical moments they'd shared; but all she found was a hard, cold glint.

"I guess we'll see you later, then," she said.

Charlie rotated his head from one side to the other, studying first the doorjamb and then the door, looking at anything other than Brigitte Dumont's eyes. If he looked there, he might believe that hurt expression; and if he let himself believe it, then he'd be lost.

He grunted agreement that he'd see her at the meeting. An awkward pause followed, during which he kept her in his peripheral vision, still unwilling to look at her face-to-face. He felt the emotional force of her shrug, her frustration and resignation.

"Welcome back to the Chalet Dumont, Mr. Battle," she said, then spun on her heel and stalked down the hall.

He should have been relieved that she had read his coldness, gotten the message so quickly. He should have been gloating over his success in letting her know that he wasn't going to fall under the spell of her charm again. He should have been relieved, gloating, but instead he ached, knowing he'd tossed aside something he desperately wanted. For the life of him, he couldn't remember why he'd ever thought wanting her was so wrong—which was exactly why he retreated into his corner suite, slammed the door as forcefully as the heavy hotel door could be slammed and, dissatisfied with the lack of noise resulting from that act, gave the security knob a savage twist.

The knob would bar a key entering the room lock. It wasn't so easy, however, to bar Brigitte Dumont from his thoughts.

BRIGITTE DELIBERATELY arrived late for the meeting. After the tense exchange with Charlie earlier, she preferred rudeness to the risk of finding herself alone with Mr. C. H. Battle.

She heard excited chatter and followed the noise to the center of the room, where Charlie knelt over the life-size soft sculpture. "The victim, I presume," she said to no one in particular.

"His name is Vincent Langton, but Nicole and I call him Uncle Vin," Jennifer reported.

"He was shot in the chest with this!" Nicole exclaimed, holding up a handgun.

Claire shivered. "Quit waving that thing around!"

"It's not real," Nicole added. "Mr. Battle got it at a toy store."

"It looks real."

"Many things look real and aren't. Like some people," Charlie stated pointedly.

For the first time since Brigitte entered the room, he looked directly at her face. The vehemence in his eyes sent a chill up her spine. He'd aimed that little barb of innuendo straight at her, cold-bloodedly, and she had no idea why. *Why? What had she done to deserve his scorn?*

"Why would a toy store stock such a thing?" Claire asked.

"It's a scale replica," Charlie replied. "Some people collect them, like dolls or horses."

"Lovely hobby," Claire remarked. "Put it down, Nicole."

"But—"

"Put it down until we need it for the mystery."

Nicole gingerly laid down the gun.

"Is it time for the blood?" Jennifer asked. She was holding a plastic bottle of red fluid.

"Not until the rug gets here," Jean-Pierre said. Turning to Brigitte, he explained, "Stephen and Claude went to get that old rug from the storeroom. The one with the paint stains. That way, the unfortunate Mr. Langton can bleed profusely."

"That should give the guests a thrill."

"Nicole and I get to help with the blood," Jennifer said.

Janet spread her hand over her rounded abdomen. "I'm not staying to watch."

Brigitte gave her a sympathetic chuckle, then sat down on the edge of the bed, since all the chairs were occupied by various Dumonts. "So, tell me more about the unfortunate Mr. Langley."

"Langton," her father corrected. "He is a close friend of Stephen's."

"They were on the same ski team," Marguerite said. "Vincent is almost like a second son to your father and me."

"That's why we call him Uncle Vin," Jennifer said.

"Much to their father's dismay," Claire said. "You see, I was madly in love with Vincent once, before I met Claude."

Brigitte had to hand it to Charlie—he'd created an intricate web of relationships between the fictional victim and the Dumont family members. "What does Claude think of that?"

"He never liked Vincent, of course," Claire replied, obviously amused by the roles into which she and her husband had been cast. "But for the sake of family unity, he tolerated him."

"Which makes him a likely suspect," Brigitte said.

"No more than Claire," Marguerite pointed out. "After all, she was the woman scorned, and Dumonts are known to be hot-blooded."

Claire sighed dramatically. "Even after all these years—"

Brigitte fixed her mother with a wry grin. "I don't suppose you had a hot affair going with the infamous Mr. Langton."

"No," Marguerite answered. "Although he did make...overtures once. But that was New Year's Eve, and he was nursing a broken heart and was inebriated. Stephen and your father took care of the situation, and he apologized after recovering from his hangover. None of us took it too seriously."

Brigitte cocked an eyebrow at her father. "Unless Père has been brooding about it, keeping his fury inside, finally working himself into a violent, uncontrollable frenzy."

"So, he's a suspect, too," Claire said. "You seem to have thought of everything, Mr. Battle." She turned to Brigitte. "Aren't you curious about your part?"

"I'm afraid to ask."

"You've got the best motive of all, Babycakes," Charlie said. "The late Vincent Langton was your betrothed."

"Your *lover!*" Nicole exclaimed, emphasizing the word.

"And you had a big fight with him in the dining room and everybody heard," Jennifer added enthusiastically.

"You *slapped* him," Nicole embellished. "And you said you *knew* he was seeing another woman."

"Vincent is emerging as a very naughty boy," Brigitte observed. "I suppose that gives me a motive, too."

"The will gives you a stronger one," Charlie said.

"Will?"

"Langton signed an amended will leaving you most of his estate when you signed the prenuptial agreement."

"A prenuptial agreement. *Quelle romantique!* That Vinnie was such a charmer!"

Charlie ignored her quip. "You're about to become a very wealthy woman, Babycakes—if you don't wind up on death row."

Jennifer's enchantment with the entire drama was obvious. "You have to kiss Fantasy Fuzz and everything so he won't try to put you in jail," she told Brigitte.

*Which, considering C. H. Battle's current attitude, is about as appealing as the prospect of sucking lemons,* Brigitte thought.

Stephen and Claude came in, each holding an end of a rolled rug, setting off a flurry of activity as Charlie tossed Vincent Langton over his shoulder in a fireman's "carry" position and everyone else scurried to move furniture so the rug could be spread out.

"If Cleopatra comes rolling out of there, you're in big trouble," Claire told Claude.

"Fine talk from a woman who's been pining after a man named Vincent," Claude parried.

"That was years ago," Claire said blithely.

Brigitte's gaze strayed to Charlie, who effortlessly held the gangly sculpture slung over his shoulder. His back was to her, and she studied the lines of his shirt as it stretched and draped over his broad muscles and remembered— though she would have preferred not to—what it felt like to be in Charlie's arms, and how effortlessly he'd lifted *her* off the ground as he'd kissed her.

That memory brought renewed disappointment over Charlie's inexplicable change of attitude. For weeks she'd lived in anticipation of seeing him again, of continuing from where they'd left off in the fitness room; of getting to know him better. Now she wished Cleopatra *had* come tumbling out of the rug; if she had, they could make her an honorary member of the Dumont family, and *she* could play Babycakes.

Realizing she was staring, Brigitte sighed and forced her gaze away from Charlie's back. How was she supposed to play Babycakes and ignore the chemistry between them? How could she kiss him in front of an audience and not remember the sweetness of having been kissed by him in private?

When the rug was spread and squared, Charlie lowered the body to the floor and set about positioning it.

"Is it time for the blood yet?" Nicole asked hopefully.

"Almost," Charlie said.

"I'm out of here," Janet announced.

Stephen rolled his eyes at his wife. "You can't stand a little fake blood, you can't bend over, you can't drink wine, you can't stand the sight of scrambled eggs—"

"And *you* can't give birth, so we're even," Janet said, grabbing his hand. "Come on, Papa. We just got a massive stock shipment in Dumontique. I'll price if you open boxes."

"I'm not sure I'm up to it," Stephen remarked. "I'm about to find out that my best friend has been murdered."

"If you start to get too broken up, just remember that sports writer he stole away from you—what was her name?"

"Samantha."

"So, you have a motive for doing in Mr. Langton, too," Brigitte said.

"A very weak one. It was a long time ago. Besides—" he stretched his arm across Janet's shoulders and grinned down at her "—good ole Vin did me a favor when he stole Samantha away from me. If he hadn't, I might have married her, and then I'd never have met Janet."

"Go ahead. Flatter me. But you're still going to open boxes," Janet said.

"Nag, nag, nag," Stephen teased.

"I don't know how you ever did without me," Janet said, as they walked toward the door.

"Now, can we do the blood?" Nicole asked.

"Yes," Charlie replied. "But we have to do it very carefully. We want it to look as though he actually bled."

"I think I'd rather wait and see the finished product with the weekenders," Marguerite Dumont said, rising.

"We should be downstairs to greet them personally as they check in anyway," Jean-Pierre reminded.

Sensing an opportune exit, Brigitte said, "I'll go with you. If the line gets too backlogged, I can work the desk."

Charlie and the girls were still experimenting with the sideways tilt of Vin's body and speculating over which direction the blood would flow from each position, but Charlie's head jerked up at Brigitte's comment. "You can't leave."

She gave him a questioning look.

"I haven't briefed you about your role in the scenario. I talked to everyone else."

"Oh. Of course." She sat down on the corner of the bed again. How could she have forgotten? She had several logistical details she needed to go over with him in order to coordinate meals and crowd distribution during the next day and a half. If she'd been working on this event for anyone but BARF, she'd have demanded more details in advance. Now, mere hours before she'd be standing in front of fifty amateur sleuths to welcome them to the Chalet Dumont, she'd been about to walk out without even asking the most fundamental questions about how the crime-scene examination would be handled.

As a Dumont, she'd been involved with the chalet and its operation all her life. While there had been no pressure on her to join the chalet's management team after finishing school, she had fulfilled the family's unstated hopes that she would find a career working alongside her parents and older siblings. She loved her job at the chalet and prided herself on performing as well as or better than any "outsider." The idea that she had let her personal involvement with Charlie distract her from her professional duties disturbed her. She expected and demanded more of herself.

Her shoulders stiffened with resolve. *Go on, Mr. Battle. Be an enigma. Be rude. Do an about-face with no explanation. Kiss me, then give me the cold shoulder. You're not going to distract me anymore. This mystery weekend is going to be a smashing success—because of you, in spite of you, or both!*

A shrill giggle drew Brigitte's attention to the center of the action, where her nieces were watching stage blood ooze over Vincent Langton's chest and drip onto the rug. "Awesome!" Nicole exclaimed. "Where do you buy this stuff?"

"Don't tell her!" Claire said urgently.

"Oh, Mom!"

"Why invite trouble?" Claire asked.

"We need some more," Jennifer informed them from the scene of the crime.

"I don't think so," Charlie said. "A little blood goes a long way, eh? Some of our participants may not be ready for too much realism."

"Wimps!" Nicole opined.

"We do *not* refer to Chalet Dumont guests as wimps, ever," Claire chided.

"Yes, Mama," Nicole said sarcastically, then scowled.

Before Claire could reprimand her, Charlie asked, "Do you girls remember what you're supposed to tell everyone when they ask you questions?"

"'We loved Uncle Vin,'" Jennifer answered. "'He brought us candy and toys when he visited.'"

"'And he treated me like an adult,'" Nicole said. "'He flirted with me.'" She giggled. "'Last Christmas he kissed me under the mistletoe and Mama didn't like it!'"

Brigitte shot her sister a wry smile. "Not only the woman scorned, but a protective mama."

"The fact that your fiancé was kissing your niece in a less-than-appropriate way did not thrill *you*, either," Charlie stated harshly. He looked at Nicole. "And what is your attitude?"

"Upset and a little scared, like there's something I don't want anyone to find out."

"Excellent."

"Why can't you tell us what we're hiding?" Nicole wanted to know.

"I'll tell you as we go along. This way, nothing will slip out prematurely, and you can focus on acting nervous."

"We shouldn't have to wait like everybody else," Nicole complained.

Charlie flashed her a smile. "The suspense will make it more fun, eh?"

Nicole's harrumph of dissatisfaction was softened by an expression of pure adolescent admiration for the man who'd made her a part of the scenario. So Nicole had fallen under his spell, too, Brigitte observed, unsure whether she wanted to warn Nicole that she was headed for heartbreak or warn Charlie what he might be letting himself in for if he encouraged the crush—even unwittingly. Finally she decided that Nicole was destined to suffer several bouts of adolescent disillusionment as an inevitable part of growing up, and Charlie was a grown man who could fend for himself. The only thing she'd gain from warning either of them was being perceived as a meddlesome busybody.

"If you girls are finished helping Mr. Battle with the blood, you should go get ready for dinner," Claire said.

"Can't we stay?" Nicole asked, and Jennifer added a pair of pleading-puppy-dog eyes to the request.

"It's only an hour and a half," Claire reminded. "It'll take you that long to do your hair."

Defeated, the girls shrugged, then told Charlie good-bye. Claire left, too, herding the girls out like a mother hen with her chicks.

Brigitte was determined not to allow the fact that she was alone with Charlie intimidate her. She was there to conduct business, and he was essential to it. Everything else was irrelevant. His fit body was irrelevant. Ditto the way his hair strayed over his forehead, making her want to feel the texture of it. Ditto that he had a charming smile when he chose to use it. Ditto that he was wearing the same after-shave he'd been wearing the last time she'd been alone with him, and the scent set off a flood of memories. Ditto that she couldn't look at his mouth and not think of the effect his kiss had had on her.

It was even irrelevant, she told herself, that he'd done an abrupt about-face with no explanation. All that was relevant was that they had fifty people coming to the chalet expecting to be enthralled, intrigued and entertained by murder, mayhem and Fantasy Fuzz—and paying dearly for the privilege.

Just in case she might be tempted to forget what was relevant and what was irrelevant, Brigitte moved from the corner of the bed to one of the chairs at the small table. "So," she said.

Charlie sat down in the other chair. Brigitte told herself that the fact his knee was so close to hers she could actually feel his body heat meant nothing. Still, she crossed her right leg over her left, jutting her left knee away from Charlie's in the process. No need to tempt fate, especially when she'd caught another whiff of his after-shave as he'd sat down.

## 7

CHARLIE WAS NOT thinking charitable thoughts about Brigitte Dumont, especially after she crossed her legs so provocatively. She had great legs. He appreciated the sleek lines of them, the alluring shading added by the taupe stockings she wore, and he badly wanted to touch them, feel their texture against his skin.

*Which was the last thing he needed to be thinking about,* he reminded himself sternly. She wasn't making it easy for him to ignore the attraction he felt for her. Everything from the sheen of her dark hair to the slightly impish upward tilt of the tip of her nose, to the glistening splendor of her lips, seemed a deliberate attempt to stir his awareness of her as a woman.

"So," he said, echoing her.

They stared awkwardly at each other. Brigitte drummed her fingers, pinkie to index, on the top of the table, then realized what she was doing and stopped with her fingers in midair, looking at her hand as though it belonged to someone else. Charlie followed her gaze to her hand, noted the pearlescent shine of her nail polish, the dainty rings she wore, the smoothness of her skin—and swallowed. Brigitte noticed the bob of his Adam's apple and tried not to let her gaze wander lower, to the broad expanse of his chest, or higher, to his craggy, uncompromising face.

Her mouth suddenly went dry, and she swallowed to moisten it so she could speak—if she could ever think of anything passably intelligent to say. Determined to end the stalemate, Brigitte focused on business. "So, who discovers the body tonight?"

"Your brother, Stephen. Vincent was his friend. When Vincent doesn't show up at dinner, Stephen comes upstairs to find out why."

"I suppose Babycakes is standing over the body wearing a lace negligee and holding a smoking gun in her hand."

"You have a negligee, don't you?" Charlie asked, trying very hard not to imagine what Brigitte would look like in one.

"No, actually. A satin teddy, maybe. But I don't think—"

"I was only joking," Charlie said humorlessly. He didn't know what a teddy was, but he was quite sure it couldn't be as sexy as the garments his mind was designing and putting on Brigitte Dumont's body. "No one is dumb enough to pick up a murder weapon and stand over a body with it."

"Not even a Babycakes?" Brigitte asked sardonically.

"The gun won't be found until tomorrow. Tonight you'll be dining with the BARF weekenders, wondering why Vincent hasn't shown up."

"Wondering if he's with his latest totsy?"

Charlie refused to be baited by her sarcasm. "It wouldn't hurt if you appeared a little antsy, checking your watch, looking at the empty seat next to you. You want the sleuths to notice that something's not quite right. Toward the end of the meal, ask Stephen if he has any idea where Vincent is or why he might be late. He and Janet will act very strange about it, and he'll be concerned enough to volunteer to check on Vincent."

"You want the weekenders to overhear?"

"Yes, so they can compare notes and discuss what they've heard later and speculate. Eventually it'll become clear that everything they might have noticed was important. Until then, they'll be trying to guess whether there's a real crisis, or whether it's part of the fake murder mystery."

"Are you going to be at dinner?"

He shook his head. "I don't want to get out of the Fantasy Fuzz character. I'll be here, as Fuzz, when the detection teams come through the scene."

"How do you want to handle that?"

"What would happen if the situation were real—if Stephen came upstairs and found his best friend murdered?"

"He'd telephone the authorities—"

"Who'd send Fuzz."

"Then he'd let my father know."

"How?"

Brigitte chewed on her bottom lip as she considered the question. While waiting for her to answer, Charlie pondered the delights of chewing on Brigitte's bottom lip. Of course, he reminded himself with bitterness, if he succumbed to that particular temptation, he'd probably find a full account of his actions, along with a Richter-scale rating of how well he'd performed, in the Sunday newspaper. Hell, she could hit the talk-show circuit if the Richter rating was high enough.

"Stephen wouldn't want to leave the room," Brigitte said. "He'd most likely call the desk and ask them to send a bellhop into the dining room with a note telling Père to come to Vincent's room immediately."

"Hmm." Charlie's forehead furrowed as he concentrated.

Brigitte felt a strong compulsion to hop onto his lap, muss his hair, kiss the tip of his nose and watch the furrows disappear as she shifted his focus from the mystery event to good old-fashioned, basic urges. Luckily she was able to thwart that compulsion by reminding herself of C. H. Battle's schizoid personality. Considering his current attitude, he'd probably leap out of his chair and send her bouncing to the floor on her behind.

"Vincent's your fiancé. Stephen would want to break the news to you before everyone else found out, wouldn't he?"

"He might. He'd tell Père to bring me upstairs in his note."

"I want him to do that," Charlie said. "Exactly that. Without telling the bellhop ahead of time. Your father will read the note, find you and tap you on the shoulder and ask you to come with him. You should act surprised and ask him, so that others can overhear, what's wrong."

"I probably wouldn't do that."

"Do what?"

"Make a fuss. If my father interrupted during a meal to tell me to come with him, I'd *know* something was up. I'd leave as unobtrusively as possible."

"Take some dramatic license," Charlie told her brusquely. "You're pretty good at that, aren't you?"

Brigitte shot him a *look*. She recognized the challenge in his rhetorical question. Challenge and hostility and a dollop of bitterness. But why? The expression in his eyes—an impenetrable coldness—reaffirmed what she heard.

He spoke without warmth. "Shortly after you come upstairs, your father will return to the dining room, explain that there's been a murder and invite the guests to try to find the murderer. Somehow they must be divided into teams."

"You mentioned that before. Five teams of ten each. I've taken two face cards out of a deck of playing cards, and we'll have one card, facedown, at each place-setting. Aces through ten of each suit will form a team named after their respective suits, and those with face cards will be called The Royals."

"Very ingenious," he said almost resentfully.

"Just doing my job," Brigitte replied curtly, with a false smile.

A long silence passed before she spoke again. "You want the teams to come through one at a time?"

"Yes. Your father can bring them up, introduce me as Fantasy Fuzz, and I'll walk them through, pointing out pertinent details. They'll want to speak to you and Stephen as soon as they leave the crime scene. Is there a conference room or someplace where you can talk to them?"

"I can arrange it." *Although I'd be furious with anyone else for not giving me advance notice.*

"Get Stephen's wife in there, too. Janet. At this point, you three are the key players. Vincent was your fiancé. He was also Stephen's best friend, and Stephen found the body. Janet is pregnant, so everyone will be concerned about the effect of the shocking news on her."

"Am I supposed to be weeping copious tears?"

"Off and on," he said. "Try to answer questions the way you would if Vincent had existed and had been murdered. You'll be devastated, naturally, and not apt to speak ill of the dead—although it should be clear you're hiding something when they grill you."

"Why would they grill me? I'm the brokenhearted girlfriend."

"They'll grill you," he told her. "Spouses and lovers—especially beautiful women—are always suspect. They'll want to know all about your relationship with Vincent. *All.* They'll ask if you were lovers."

"How should I respond to that?"

"Be evasive. Embarrassed. Shrug and say, 'Well, we *were* engaged to be married.'"

He wasn't trying to be funny, but Brigitte had to bite her lip to keep from laughing aloud at his falsetto imitation and the imaginary handkerchief he flapped in the air. "In other words, I'm supposed to admit that he and I were lovers by avoiding any direct answers."

"That should be easy enough for a woman of your talents."

On the surface it sounded like a compliment, but Brigitte recognized the insult in the remark—not sarcasm, which would indicate that Charlie didn't believe she had talent; but condemnation, as though he acknowledged her talent and found it offensive.

"They'll ask if you were faithful to Vincent and if he was faithful to you. While you won't come right out and accuse Vincent of having a lover, you should act so upset by the question of his fidelity that the sleuths are suspicious. And you should try to give each team the same general information.

"Each team will have a five-minute briefing and then ten minutes to examine the crime scene. Then they can spend fifteen minutes with you and Janet and Stephen while the next team is at the crime scene, and so on."

"We're going to have to have something to entertain the last teams during the hours they're waiting for their turn at the crime scene," Brigitte thought aloud, automatically concentrating on the practical considerations of crowd management. "We're going to sing the 'Ballad of Fantasy Fuzz' before dinner. Claire can lead them through a few more choruses if they get restless."

"They'll be too busy pumping everyone for information about the victim to get restless," Charlie pointed out. "Claire will tell them he was your fiancé. Claude will manage to let them know he didn't like Vincent, and the girls will remember Uncle Vin fondly."

"And the infamous mistletoe kiss," Brigitte said. The genius of the plotting gave her goose pimples—the kind a person gets when she realizes something's going to turn out even better than expected. "I knew this murder-mystery idea would be fun," she told Charlie. "But I hadn't imagined how intriguing it would be. You're going to have everyone guessing and leaping to wild conclusions. I'm impressed, Charlie."

Her use of his first name disturbed him. It sounded too intimate on her lips; too personal, too sincere. It made Charlie want to hear that same name whispered by that same voice under different circumstances.

Charlie didn't want to want to hear that voice saying his name. Irritated with himself, for wanting to hear that voice say his name again, he asked gruffly, "So that's why BARF wanted a scenario by C. H. Battle, isn't it?"

The question smacked of resentment, and Brigitte wondered why. Did he feel he'd been pressured into writing the scenario? That didn't make any sense. They'd asked him politely, and he'd agreed. How could he possibly resent a polite request?

Brigitte didn't see any advantage in telling him that she'd been enthusiastic about his participation because she'd considered his name a draw. Besides, since she wasn't a *Fantasy Fuzz* reader, it had never occurred to her that story lines revolving around a suspect called Babycakes could be particularly ingenious.

"Should we involve any of the staff?" she asked, after a prolonged silence.

"How well do they know the family? Would, say, the bartender in your nightclub recognize you?"

"Absolutely."

"Would he know you were engaged?"

"Are you kidding? This is the Chalet Dumont. None of the Dumonts can sneeze without the staff saying *gesundheit*."

"We should brief the bartender, then. Vincent frequented the bar with assorted members of the family or alone. Vincent liked the booze."

"Some charming guy you almost married me off to!"

"Can you feed it into your computer that Vincent checked in on Thursday and instructed the desk clerks to give out that information if asked?"

Brigitte sighed. "That's contrary to standard policy, you know. But I suppose since it's only a game—"

"What about the maid who cleans this floor? She'd be curious about his room because of his involvement with you, wouldn't she?"

"Curious?" Brigitte asked.

"She'd be on the lookout for signs that you'd been there—your hairbrush, maybe. An extra toothbrush. A nightie. Your perfume on the sheets."

"Probably." Frowning, Brigitte agreed. "Unfortunately. Of course, any of our maids would be fired on the spot if we caught her gossiping about a guest. But, as you say, she'd be curious. I suppose we could brief her and tell her what you'd want her to reveal. After all, a man has been murdered."

"Good. She can suggest the idea of a second woman in Vincent's life."

"I don't know what I ever saw in the two-timing, boozing weasel."

"In a word, money."

Brigitte scowled at him. "If he was so rich—and he obviously didn't care enough about me to be faithful—what did he want with me?"

Charlie hesitated before answering. Looking at her, he was tempted to tell her all the things a man might want her for. He was doing a little wanting himself at the moment. Instead, he said, "Open your eyes, Babycakes. He was a skier. This is a ski lodge. If he married you, he could loll around here skiing, flirting and swilling good whiskey for the rest of his life without anyone asking him why he didn't have a real job. And he'd be tapping into the prestige of the Dumont name."

"No wonder someone shot him," Brigitte replied. "What a louse! Who did it, by the way?"

"There will be a dramatic confession Sunday morning," Charlie said.

Brigitte gave him an exasperated frown. "You can't even tell me?"

Charlie chortled softly. "You sound like your niece."

But she wasn't her niece, and she wasn't thirteen. She was Brigitte Dumont, a full-grown woman, and Charlie couldn't have been more aware of it if she'd been wearing a flashing neon sign announcing the fact. Whereas Nicole had sounded petulant and rebellious when she'd protested, Brigitte projected a pouty sexuality that challenged a man into flexing muscles and proving his dominance. Most of all, it made him want to kiss her. Not too gently, either—at least until she began kissing him back, melting against him in boneless surrender—

*Damn it, why did he have to kiss her in the first place?* He'd been yearning, craving something all his adult life without knowing what it was. Now that he'd seen, smelled, *tasted* Brigitte Dumont, felt her in his arms, he knew. And it was so much worse and more poignant now that he knew exactly what he craved. The wanting had been far easier to bear when it was just a vague frustration. Now it was a focused longing, sharper than intense pain.

Did it matter so much that she was indiscreet? That their time alone had meant nothing more personal to her than an hour at a shopping mall? If he could kiss her again, hold her, feel those delicious breasts crushed against his chest, the soft blossoming of her mouth under his, would it matter so much that it was only for the moment? People thought he was such a big deal since he'd become famous. Maybe it was time he cashed in on his celebrity, sat back and enjoyed the fringe benefits, nibbled at the buffet—

"Come on," Brigitte said, springing to her feet.

Charlie had been so caught up in his desire for her that he'd thoroughly tuned out. "Huh?"

"If we go to the bar now, we can beat the predinner rush. I'll buy you a drink. Who knows? Maybe if I ply you with liquor, you'll tell me who wasted the louse I almost married."

"Don't count on it," he replied. "I'm a sullen drunk."

There were only a handful of guests in San Sousi, the Chalet Dumont's glitzy night club, when Brigitte and Charlie walked in. Brigitte guided Charlie straight to the chrome-trimmed bar and motioned for the bartender, who flashed her a wide smile as he approached. Standing opposite them, he asked, "Brigitte. H'lo. What can I do for you?"

"Jake, this is C. H. Battle. He needs to talk to you about the murder-mystery event that starts tonight. Charlie, this is Jake."

Jake leaned across the bar to shake hands. "You the Fantasy Fuzz guy?"

Charlie nodded.

Brigitte had moved to the opening at the far end of the bar and stepped behind it. She spread her hand over Jake's beefy forearm. "Go on. I'll work the bar while you two talk."

"Anything you say, boss," Jake said.

Brigitte watched the two men settle at an out-of-the-way table in the back corner of the long narrow room, then turned her attention to the clutter of bottles on the work counter in front of her, hoping no one would want anything too complicated.

Charlie briefly outlined the mystery scenario and gave Jake a quick character assessment of the murdered man. "You should act a little resentful of this Vincent character because of the way he treated Brigitte," he instructed. "Like maybe you care about her, and didn't like seeing her treated badly. You could even be a little in love with her."

"That won't take much acting," Jake said.

Jake was in his late twenties, with long hair slicked into a ponytail and a physique that would enable him to serve as bouncer as well as bartender if the need arose. The expression in his eyes undermined his tough-guy demeanor. Charlie followed his gaze to the bar, where Brigitte was chatting animatedly with a patron while mixing a drink. The silver-blue neon tubing that spelled out San Sousi in front of the mirror lining the wall behind the bar cast an ethereal glow that made her appear slightly ghost-like . . . and hauntingly beautiful.

"You two got something going?" Charlie asked, a little afraid of the answer.

"You mean beyond the fact that I imagine making her the mother of my children every time I see her? Get real. She's not just management, she's the big boss's daughter."

Charlie felt he'd established enough masculine rapport to ask, "You ever try?"

"Only in my dreams. I'm just the hired help around here."

"She make a big deal of that?"

"Brigitte? Hell, no. She's always just like she is over there right now. Smiling. Friendly. She's that way with everybody."

"Then why haven't you tried?"

Jake chortled. "Because I like my job, and I like my heart in one piece. Suppose it happened. Suppose she gave me a tumble and the earth moved and fireworks went off. In the end, she'd still be a Dumont, and I'd still be the hired help." He slowly shook his head from side to side. "It sure doesn't hurt to look. She's easy on the eyes, eh?"

"That she is," Charlie agreed. *Far too easy. So easy that the sight of her made his body ache with desire.* "She have lots of men?" he asked.

Jake took a sip of cola while he considered the question. "The men sniff around," he finally answered, "but she doesn't let them get too close, if you know what I mean."

*I got close to her,* Charlie thought fiercely. Or, at least, he thought he had. His resentment at her betrayal washed over him in a fresh wave of disappointment and regret over what might have been. He reminded himself that he was there to plot an intriguing murder and *not* to pry into Brigitte Dumont's love life—no matter how consumed by curiosity he was.

"So you've seen this Vincent character in the bar often, every time he's been at the hotel," he instructed Jake. "He drank a lot and he flirted a lot, which made you want to punch him in the teeth. He was here this afternoon until Brigitte arrived. She stayed only long enough for him to settle his tab and they left together. They didn't look happy. And last night, for a few minutes Claire came in and sat down next to him. You thought that was strange, since Claire rarely comes into the bar, and never without Claude. So you watched them. They were very involved in whatever they were talking about, and you wondered if something was wrong. Claire seemed agitated. Then she left, and you forgot all about it. You got that? Don't volunteer it, but if anyone asks, let them lead you into it."

"Gotcha," Jake said. "My lips are sealed until they ask. Then I'm a blabbermouth." Something at the bar captured his attention and he rose from his chair, extending his hand to Charlie as he stood. "Nice meeting you, Mr. Battle, but I'd better get back to work. That guy who just walked in drinks Harvey Wallbangers, and Brigitte's just liable to make them with tequila or something—not that anyone would care, if she served it up with a smile."

Charlie stood as Brigitte approached the table. "Good news," she announced. "I called one of our maids and she agreed to come back in tonight and talk to the teams. If you brief her, she can answer questions in the bar area of the suite before the teams come downstairs to the conference room. Angie will be perfect for the part. She's always chattering and laughing. She'll relate very easily to the sleuths."

"Excellent."

"If we're finished with all this nefarious crime planning for the time being, I could feed Vincent's registration data into the computer now."

"I need to talk to the pastry chef," Charlie said. "I'd like to compliment him on the Babycakes cake he did last time I was here."

"He'll be thrilled. He's working on a similar cake for tonight. I'll walk you into the kitchens."

Charlie was fascinated by the process of piping icing through the various metal tips to produce frosting designs. Sensing that he'd been assigned center stage in front of none other than the creator of *Fantasy Fuzz*, Gérard launched into a flamboyant explanation of the importance of getting the icing to the right consistency and using just the right pressure on the bags to control the width of the icing flow, and soon had Charlie practicing squibbles and scrollwork on a sheet of wax paper.

Brigitte watched. They created an incongruous tableau: large, strong Charlie with hands big enough to span a typical layer cake trying to manipulate a bulging icing-filled parchment bag with a concentration so fierce that it furrowed his forehead, and amiable little cherubic Gérard demonstrating with stubby fingers how to control the icing designs.

When Gérard started dropping hints that Charlie might want to pipe a likeness of Fantasy Fuzz on the center of the cake that would be served to the Death at the Dumont guests, Brigitte retreated, leaving them absorbed in their craft and carrying with her the image of Charlie's broad shoulder muscles straining against the cloth of his shirt as he bent over the work counter.

# 8

BRIGITTE STRETCHED her arms across the conference table in front of her and bent over to rest her forehead against the tabletop. She released a long, weary sigh. "I never realized grief could be so exhausting."

"Or shock," Janet agreed. "If I'd had to pat my tummy one minute longer, I'd have gone running from the room genuinely hysterical."

"The first three times we went through the routine weren't so bad, but the last two . : ." Stephen grumbled. "I swear I wanted to punch out that last guy. Had there ever been 'anything *funny*' between Vincent and me—like a torrid affair!"

"That was one of the lawyers," Brigitte explained. "He and three of his cohorts from the same firm traded cards until each of them had a different suit so they could be on different teams. They're a little competitive."

"I should have known he was a lawyer," Stephen replied. "He had a courtroom attitude."

"You're just tired," Janet said, patting his arm. "Besides, you set him straight."

"Damned right," Stephen said.

"Now that we're alone, are you going to tell me what really happened to your hand?" Brigitte asked.

Stephen held up his right hand and admired Charlie's artwork. "Charlie painted it with food coloring he borrowed from Gérard. Really looks bruised, doesn't it?"

"It fooled me," Brigitte told him.

"Your reaction was priceless," Stephen said. "Charlie told me just to let people notice naturally and tell them I'd crushed it between some boxes in Dumontique. When you asked what was heavy enough to bruise my hand that way and I told you I couldn't remember what I'd been unpacking, everyone at the table sprang to attention."

"Everyone obviously thinks you punched Vincent out, since his face was bruised up, but you stuck to that flimsy box story."

"Charlie told him to," Janet said. "I guess we'll find out why he beat up his best friend at tomorrow morning's briefing." She gave her husband a sardonic look. "Do you suppose it was a lovers' quarrel?"

"Perish the thought!"

"I wonder if you shot him, too," Janet added, at the tail end of a yawn.

"There'll be a dramatic confession Sunday morning," Brigitte announced, mimicking Charlie. "I wonder when he'll brief the person who's supposed to make this dramatic confession."

"Probably Sunday morning," Stephen speculated. "He seems adamant about keeping the suspense high, even among the players. Until then, you're the only one who can sleep with an easy conscience."

"Why me?"

"Because Babycakes is never guilty."

"Of murder, maybe," Brigitte said.

"Well, I, for one, am going to sleep just fine," Janet declared, standing and stretching stiffly. "If I'm guilty, so be it. Although why I'd want to kill Stephen's best friend is beyond me."

"Because of the 'funny' stuff?" Brigitte suggested, earning a scowl from her brother. Stephen had a tendency to be grumpy when he was tired. Actually, Stephen had a tendency to be grumpy, period.

"Come on," Janet said, taking Stephen's hand and guiding his arm across her shoulders. "You can help a tired, pregnant lady to bed."

"Only if I can crawl in with you."

"Obviously you already did that!" Brigitte teased, letting her gaze land on Janet's puffy midsection.

Janet looked at Brigitte. "Are you going down to the bar to mingle?"

"That would hardly be suitable conduct for the grieving fiancée. I'm going to return to the scene of the crime and see if our detective survived the stampede of the curious hordes."

Janet raised an eyebrow. "Your interest is purely professional, of course?"

"Purely," Brigitte replied, although she knew it was a lie. Her mouth was dry with the anticipation of being alone with Charlie. She was going to him as special-events coordinator for the Chalet Dumont, but in her heart she wished she could walk into the suite and discover the shy, charming man she'd danced with in the fitness room instead of the boor who'd shown up this afternoon. It was dangerous to hope—since he was unpredictable at best— but her heart chose not to heed the warning, remembering the expression in his eyes after he'd kissed her, the intensity in his voice as he told her that if she looked at him that way again, he'd never be able to let her go.

The memory of that moment was vivid in Brigitte's mind as she knocked at the door to the "murder" suite. The door opened with a sudden whoosh and she found herself nose to chest with the creator of Fantasy Fuzz. She watched his features tauten, his expression close up. Sensing the wall he erected between them, she wanted to flail at his broad chest and demand to know how he could be as warm as a woolly teddy bear one night and as cool and remote as an Arctic penguin the next time she saw him.

*Why?* The question pierced her chest like a dagger, but she was unable to voice it. The wall was too intimidating. "I, uh, wondered how everything went up here," she said, brushing past him into the room.

"Smooth as a baby's behind," Charlie replied. "Our weekend detectives were chomping at the bit for information. One of the men had an instant camera, and he was taking pictures from every angle."

"He took pictures of Stephen's hand, too," Brigitte said. "And questions! I don't know how they thought them all up."

"Lord, yes! I thought I was going to get tongue-tied answering them all."

Stunned, Brigitte followed the female voice to the sofa in the seating area near the victim. "Angie!" she exclaimed, trying to hide her surprise at finding the maid still there. "I didn't see you sitting there."

"I clocked out as soon as the last of the detectives left," Angie explained quickly. "But I said something about how all the questions had made my throat dry, and Charlie and me decided to have an unwinder."

"Oh," Brigitte replied, taking in the broader picture of the sweating drink glasses, cola cans and individual-serving liquor bottles on the coffee table.

"We found the booze in the bar cabinet," Charlie said. "You can bill my room."

"Don't be silly," Brigitte told him. "You're our special guest. I'll just leave a note for the maid to restock tomorrow."

"Why don't you join us?" Charlie suggested.

"I . . . well, if there's any white wine, sure. Why not?"

She sat in a chair facing the coffee table, consumed with curiosity about what she'd interrupted. So far, Angie had clarified that she'd clocked out and wasn't snorkeling on Chalet Dumont time, and Charlie had offered to pay for the liquor. However, neither of them had the guilty, embarrassed air of potential lovers caught with their pants unzipped.

"What kind of questions did they ask you?" she asked Angie.

"You name it, they asked it. Did I notice anything unusual about the room when I made it up this morning? Did I think Mr. Langton had any visitors, and why? Did I see anyone going in or out of the room? Had I met Mr. Langton? Did I notice anything out of place or peculiar now, compared to the way I left the room. I mean, other than Mr. Langton sprawled out in the middle of the floor, deader than a mackerel."

Brigitte studied Angie as she spoke. She was a large woman, tall and full-bodied. In her late thirties at least, Brigitte guessed. Her hair was blond, obviously colored—to cover gray, perhaps—and worn in curls produced by a permanent rather than nature. Her ready smile revealed large, rather crooked teeth. Brigitte had never looked at her as a potential rival for a man's affection. She supposed a man might find her attractive in a flaunting-it kind of way; and she had an appealing personality. If called upon to pair her with someone, though, Brigitte would have linked her with someone older and equally gregarious—a salesman, perhaps, rather than an introvert like Charlie, who was at least five years her junior.

But then, Brigitte thought, stifling a frown, she was hardly an expert on Charlie Battle. Perhaps buxom blondes were his type. Apparently petite brunettes didn't hold his attention for long.

"What information did you give them?" she asked, to keep Angie talking. She regretted her decision to stay, and if she hadn't mentioned wine and Charlie hadn't found a half-pint bottle that was now submerged in the ice bucket, she would have found some way to beat a hasty retreat.

"Just what Mr. Battle told me to say," Angie replied. "That the bed looked like it had been unmade and remade—and rather poorly, since I fixed it this morning—and that there had been a woman here last night—probably you, since you were engaged to the man. That was okay, wasn't it?"

Brigitte shrugged. "That's the story."

"This whole thing is so much *fun*," Angie went on. "And you get to play Babycakes. That must be so *exciting*."

Brigitte couldn't muster as much enthusiasm as she'd have liked. "It's definitely something to write about in my diary."

"The entire staff is so curious about it. There's a betting pool starting at the dormitory over who did it."

Brigitte raised her eyebrows. "What's the general consensus?"

"Well," Angie began, "most of the men say it was you, because you were engaged to him. But the people who are into *Fantasy Fuzz* say that's impossible because Babycakes is never guilty—no matter how guilty she looks. So now the betting's on your brother. When they heard about his hand, and the corpse having a busted jaw—" She turned to Charlie, who'd taken a seat opposite Brigitte's. "You wouldn't want to give me a little inside information, would you, so I could pick up a few bucks?"

"Sorry," Charlie said, with an apologetic shrug.

"Even the players don't know," Brigitte added.

"No fooling? Well, I guess that means everyone has an equal chance of guessing."

Brigitte leaned forward and took the wine out of the ice bucket, emptied it into the glass Charlie had brought for her and took a sip. "Thank you for staying, Angie."

"Wouldn't've missed it," Angie replied, and giggled. "I would have done it without pay—not that I'm not glad to get the extra hours. I'll be able to send a little extra to my daughter, you know."

Brigitte didn't know, and thought that perhaps she should. "You have a daughter?"

Angie nodded. "She's a freshman up at the university. Works full-time, goes to school full-time. I send her whatever I can to make it a little easier on her. She wants to be a biologist."

"You must be proud of her."

"Sure am." Finishing off her rum and coke, Angie put her empty glass on the coffee table and sighed. "It's been fun, folks, but I'm calling it a night. Everyone in the dorm is going to have to know what went on, and I've got to be at work early tomorrow morning."

Charlie walked with her to the door. He didn't return to his seat right away, but leaned against the bar and crossed his arms over his waist and looked at Brigitte. Aware of his gaze on her, she took another sip of her wine and paused deliberately before saying, "I'm sorry if I interrupted something."

It was the second time she'd lied that night.

"You didn't." It hadn't even occurred to him.

"Good." She knew her smile betrayed her relief, but couldn't control it.

Charlie didn't want to trust the smile, but couldn't keep from grinning back at her.

"I thought . . ." Brigitte began, then faltered. She took a breath and started over. "I need to know if there's anything special we need to do when we break down the crime scene. We have someone booked into this suite at noon tomorrow."

"We're finished in here."

"We can stash the body in my office until we set up the display of auction items."

"I'll carry him down for you," Charlie offered.

Brigitte shook her head. "You'd be too conspicuous. I'll call for a bellboy and a rack. We'll cover old Vin with a sheet, and take him down in the service elevator."

Charlie nodded, and a silence fell between them.

"Charlie?"

Her voice was soft, close to a whisper, and Charlie steeled himself against the effect his name on her lips had on his senses. He grunted, "Huh?"

She'd been on the verge of asking him what had happened to change his attitude toward her. For a moment, when he'd grinned at her, she'd detected a softening, a weakening of his defenses, but now that hard, closed expression was back in his eyes. He'd slammed the wall back into place.

"I can take care of this," she said. "You don't have to stick around."

Charlie wanted to stick around. His chest hurt from holding his emotions in check. His arms ached with the need to embrace her. He yearned to cross the space that separated them and pull her close and anchor her there until the lush pleasure of fulfillment eased the ache of denial.

Brigitte waited for what seemed an eternity for him to say or do something besides just stand there looking at her *that way.* She remembered the sensation of his mouth on hers, of his strength enveloping her. Then she remembered the magazine article, and the quote, *"He had this thing he did with his eyes."*

"Really," she said, as imperiously as possible. "I can handle this." A fake body. An old rug. Those things were easy. It was being alone with this remote stranger called C. H. Battle she couldn't deal with.

He had been dismissed. So Charlie fled the room with little more than a nod and a mumbled farewell. For a while he experienced the relief of a man who'd just narrowly escaped death or worse: Indignity. Exposure. Humiliation.

Then came the letdown. He was safe, but he was alone. Again. It seemed to him that he'd always been alone, but the loneliness had never been so painful nor felt so absolute. The feeling of isolation had never been so pervasive or unrelenting.

Standing outside Charlie's door, Brigitte buried her face in her hands and groaned and wondered how she would get through the weekend. As Babycakes, she'd eventually have to play the vamp with Fuzz. She'd have to flirt and cajole and seduce. She'd have to *kiss* him.

God, how was she going to kiss him in front of fifty people and then act as though it didn't mean a thing to her?

Everything would have been much simpler, she realized in a flash of self-enlightenment, if she hadn't fallen head over heels in love with Mr. C. H. Battle.

## 9

BRIGITTE OBSERVED the commotion at breakfast the next morning, created by her nieces. With suppressed amusement, Nicole and Jennifer began with an exchange of pointed, hostile looks, and proceeded to argue. Heads were turned, ears keenly attuned by the time Jennifer stood and shoved her chair back with such force that it tumbled backward with a crash. Nicole shot her younger sister a homicidal glare and said accusingly, "You promised."

"I have to!" Jennifer replied. "It's too dangerous." She stalked over to her mother, who was seated at a table across the room. Reaching her, Jennifer leaned and whispered something in her ear.

"Oh, God! No," Claire exclaimed. She looked at her husband and said his name as she tossed her napkin on the table, leaped up and scurried toward Nicole with Claude on her heels. Catching sight of Detective Fantasy Fuzz, who'd been strategically seated at a central table, she said, "You should know about this."

Fuzz rose and followed her to where Nicole was seated. Claire whispered in Nicole's ear and Nicole, with childish petulance, grabbed the tote bag she'd been using as a purse and walked out of the room with her parents and the great Detective Fuzz.

Brigitte noted the fervor of her fellow spectators with satisfaction. Her nieces had played their roles flawlessly. Claire, and even Claude, had shown just enough panic and parental concern.

Jennifer was now exactly where she wanted to be—that is, at center stage surrounded by an audience hanging on her every word. Although it was impossible for all fifty of the guests to get close enough to hear her at once, the word *gun* echoed swiftly throughout the room, and the atmosphere fairly hummed with the excitement of the guest sleuths over this new—and undoubtedly significant—development.

Death at the Dumont promised to be a roaring success if the mystery managed to sustain this level of excitement throughout its unfolding. Brigitte could take professional satisfaction from that, no matter how devastating the involvement with C. H. Battle had been to her personally.

The early-morning briefing had been torturous for her. She'd been aware of Charlie the whole time—the tone of his voice as he briefed everyone on their parts for the day, the animation in his face as he patiently stressed to the girls how they were to act at breakfast, the coldness in his eyes every time he was forced to look at her. He'd ignored her whenever possible, looking past her and around her at the other members of her family. To them, he'd been cordial; to her, curt.

She thought maybe she was being paranoid or oversensitive, but Stephen hung back as everyone filed out of the room and asked, "He's not still brooding about your cartoonist crack, is he?"

She shrugged, pleading ignorance. "I thought I was just imagining it."

Stephen's frown told her he wasn't buying her story.

"Just drop it," she said, finality in the tone of her voice. She didn't want to talk to anyone about Charlie—what was she supposed to say? *We spent a pleasant hour together and I fell in love. He drew cartoons telling me it was meaningful to him, then showed up treating me as though I were a menace to polite society.* Stephen would think her elevator wasn't going to the top floor; she suspected as much when she thought about it analytically.

Within minutes, Detective Fuzz returned to the dining room with his entourage and announced that a handgun had been found near the scene of the homicide. He offered to answer questions, press-conference style, and asked all the members of the Dumont family to come to the bandstand, to be available for questioning.

The amateur investigators wanted to know everything at once. Where was the gun found, and by whom? What kind of gun was it? Was it the murder weapon?

Charlie listened to the barrage, then made a blanket statement: "Mr. Dumont's granddaughter, Nicole Silvain, found the weapon in the hollow pedestal of an ashtray next to the elevator on the floor of the murder suite. It is a nine-millimeter German-made semiautomatic. The preliminary report on the body indicated that the wound was inflicted by a bullet between .22 caliber and .38 caliber in circumference. Until the bullet is removed from the body and examined by ballistics experts, we have no way of knowing exactly what size the bullet is. However, the wound inflicted by a nine-millimeter bullet would create the size of wound in Vincent Langton's chest."

They wanted to know when Nicole had found the gun, and how. Charlie let her take the mike and answer for herself. "I found it last night." She looked at Claire as though seeking reassurance. Brigitte couldn't help but feel proud of her performance.

Claire nodded, and Nicole continued. "Mama wouldn't let me in the room with the body, but I went up to the fourth floor, and when I got off the elevator, I noticed that the ashtray was crooked, and when I tried to fix it, I heard something go clunk in the bottom, and when I looked inside, I saw the gun, and then I put it in my tote bag."

"We have already prepared the ashtrays from the fourth floor to be taken to the forensics lab," Charlie interjected, in an official voice. "However, the ashtrays throughout the hotel are identical, should you wish to examine one to get an idea of how they're made."

"Why didn't you show the gun to someone?" The question came from one of the attorneys in the crowd.

"I was scared."

Charlie, as Fuzz, draped his arm across Nicole's shoulders, and asked gently, "Why were you so scared, honey?"

Nicole buried her face against Fuzz's trademark jacket, but Brigitte noticed with wry amusement and pride that the girl managed to speak into the microphone when she responded to his question. "Because somebody shot Uncle Vin, and—"

"Do you recognize this gun, Nicole?" Fuzz asked firmly. "Is that what scared you about it? You know who it belongs to, don't you?"

"No!" Nicole cried, and buried her face again, issuing forth a sob that would have impressed Cecil B. deMille himself.

Keeping his arm around Nicole, Charlie turned to Brigitte with a less benevolent attitude. "What about you, Babycakes? This gun look familiar?"

It was the first time he'd called her Babycakes, and the weekenders responded with a blend of gasps, applause, chuckles and cheers. Brigitte waited for silence before answering. "I don't know anything about—" She paused, milking the scene before completing the sentence with a rush of breath: "Guns."

"Sure, Babycakes," Fuzz growled back, then settled his gaze on Stephen. "What about you, Dumont? You a collector?"

"I've never even fired a handgun," Stephen replied.

"And your friend, Vincent? Was he into collectibles?"

"Not that I know of."

"The only weapon Vincent owned was an oriental ceremonial saber," Brigitte said. "It's above the mantel in his house. It was long, and shiny and—" Again she paused for dramatic effect, and then added suggestively, "*Symbolic*, you know."

"Thanks for the tip, Babycakes," Fuzz said, cocking an eyebrow at her as the audience tittered appreciatively. The remark had been improvised. Charlie turned his most intimidating interrogator's glare on Claire. "And you, Mrs. Silvain. Do you recognize this weapon? Do you or your husband—?"

Marguerite Dumont stepped forward unexpectedly. "May I take a closer look at that gun?"

Fuzz dangled the plastic bag in front of her. Nicole rushed from his arms into her mother's when he moved.

"The owner of this gun knows nothing about the killing," Mrs. Dumont announced, after studying it from several angles.

"You sound very sure," Fuzz said.

"I ought to be," Mrs. Dumont replied, squaring her shoulders. "You see, the gun belongs to me."

The audience gasped.

"It belonged to my father," Mrs. Dumont continued. "It was a war souvenir. You see the design etched into the butt? It's unique. And unmistakable."

"Who knew about this gun?" Fuzz asked.

Marguerite Dumont appeared to give the question careful thought. "My husband and I, and my children. I doubt Jennifer or Nicole knew of its existence. I did not keep it on display. I had no interest in it. I kept it only for sentiment."

"Where did you keep it?"

"In the drawer of my china hutch, under my mother's hand-embroidered linen tablecloth. I never use the tablecloth, either, but sometimes . . . I like to look at it."

"Where is this hutch?" Fuzz pressed.

"In our private suite."

"So only your immediate family would have had access to it and knowledge of it?"

Mrs. Dumont appeared panicked, then quickly recovered to reply, "That's not entirely true, Detective Fuzz. Housekeeping cleans our suite twice a week. Any of the maids who went there might have found the gun and taken it and given it to anyone. It might have been valuable. They might have taken it to sell it. It could have been missing for months."

"Was the gun loaded?"

"I am not fool enough to keep a loaded gun. There was a box of ammunition, though. My father decided to fire off some rounds one New Year's Eve, and he had to buy an entire box of bullets. I don't think the gun has been loaded or fired since."

"You're wrong, Mrs. Dumont," Fuzz said emphatically. "It seems to have been fired again, and very recently."

"You do not seriously think this could be the murder weapon!" Mrs. Dumont protested.

"Time will tell," Fuzz replied gravely. "Time will tell, Mrs. Dumont."

Charlie kept the group entertained for a while, letting them watch him fingerprint Jennifer and Nicole, both of whom had supposedly touched the gun. With sets of the girls' prints, he explained, the technician wouldn't have to waste time trying to identify prints that were inconsequential to the crime. Then he ducked out to spend time at the police lab, leaving Brigitte and her family at the mercy of the weekenders, who fired questions at them at a merciless pace, hoping to extract some revealing or, preferably, condemning information.

Miraculously, Detective Fuzz reappeared just as everyone was finishing lunch, to announce that the bullet removed from Vincent Langton's chest was, indeed, a nine-millimeter, and could have been fired from the gun

found in the ashtray. They wouldn't know for sure until
the lab boys finished dusting the gun for prints and released it to the ballistics team.

The autopsy report wasn't yet ready, but the coroner
had confided to Fuzz—and Fuzz now confided to his fellow detectives—that the chest wound inflicted by a handgun fired at close range had been confirmed as the cause
of death. The bruising on the victim's face and additional
bruising found in the area of his ribs had occurred several
hours prior to the shooting.

The amateur sleuths were able to wheedle out of him
that the bullet had been fired at a level trajectory, suggesting, though not proving, that the perpetrator was ap-
proximately the same height as the victim.

"So you think the murderer was a man?" asked an as-
tute amateur.

"Mr. Langton was five feet ten inches tall," Fuzz replied. "A woman of average height wearing shoes with
three-inch heels could conceivably have fired the shot at
what would be construed as a level trajectory." He gave
Brigitte a hard stare. "You're about average in height,
aren't you, Babycakes?"

"I haven't measured lately," Brigitte returned. "You're
not packing a . . . *yardstick*, are you, detective?"

It was a vintage Babycakes line. Charlie might have admired her ingenuity if he hadn't felt a flush rising from his
neck to creep over his face as scattered applause and a
couple of catcalls sounded in the crowd.

He gritted his teeth against the humiliation of that heat.
This never happened to Detective Fantasy Fuzz. But then,
Fantasy had never dealt with Brigitte Dumont. Which was
fortunate, Charlie thought grimly, since Fantasy Fuzz
would soon lose his macho edge if he went around blush-
ing.

Concentrating on what Fantasy *would* do, he looked
Brigitte over, letting his gaze rove lazily from her head to

her toes, lingering suggestively on some of her finer features along the way. "Five-five," he speculated. "Give or take an inch."

Brigitte seethed as she searched for an appropriate comeback. He *would* look at her that way *now*, in front of fifty nosy amateur detectives and her entire family! "I like a man who pays attention to details," she crooned.

"Just part of my job, Babycakes. Just part of my job."

"IF I WEREN'T with child, this would be a shot of hard liquor," Janet said, pushing an ice cube through her ginger ale with her fingertip.

"The day we've had would have turned Carry Nation from a Prohibitionist to a tippler," Brigitte agreed, popping two aspirin into her mouth. She chased them with white wine.

The two had managed to evade the sleuths long enough to escape into Janet and Stephen's suite for a few minutes' respite from the mayhem that had followed the murder.

"The guests are really getting into the intrigue," Brigitte commented.

"'Into' it?" Janet repeated. "I got so sick of everyone asking me about Stephen's hand, I actually told one of the weekenders that I smashed it with a rolling pin during an argument."

"You didn't!"

Janet giggled. "I did! And the most amazing thing is, they believed me. They were sure they'd found a whole new avenue to explore."

"One of those obnoxious attorneys tried to ply me with liquor and pump me for information. He had the nerve to ask if Vincent and I had been into anything kinky. I managed to get away before he attempted an overt seduction."

"Three people asked me how tall I am," Janet said. "By the way, do you wear red lace panties?"

"They're asking you that, too?"

"Apparently Angie and the good detective found a pair in the bedding in Vincent's room. If they're not yours, then there's a good possibility Vincent was being a bad boy shortly before he became a crime statistic."

"The man was a real louse," Brigitte remarked, then took a sip of wine. "The girls were very convincing in the gun scenario, weren't they?"

"Yes. You should have heard Nicole telling one of her friends about it on the telephone. She was gushing. And the main thrust of the story was that she had been *hugged* by C. H. Battle and almost fainted from the ecstasy."

"Saints preserve us!" Brigitte exclaimed. "It's rabid puppy love."

"Speaking of C. H. Battle—" Janet interjected.

"I wasn't aware we were speaking of C. H. Battle," Brigitte said coolly. "I could have sworn we were talking about Nicole, who was speaking of C. H. Battle."

"He's wonderful as Fuzz. The crowd is eating it up."

"They pays their money, they gets their fun."

"Come on, Brigitte. We're alone. It's obvious something's going on between the two of you."

"Murder."

"Humph! The way he looks at you!"

"Those looks are his specialty," Brigitte replied. "Didn't you read Donna's article? He perfected the smoldering leer in college."

"You're the only one he seems to be leering at around here," Janet pointed out. "He couldn't take his eyes off you when you were dancing that night."

"Dancing?" Brigitte snapped, wondering how much Janet knew.

"The soft shoe with Père. At Family Night. Stephen noticed."

"Stephen's always imagining that men have dishonorable intentions about me," Brigitte said. "That's just the kind of big brother he is."

"Who said anything about dishonorable intentions?" Janet countered. "The man is attracted to you, and it looks awfully two-sided."

Brigitte set her empty wineglass on the table. "Is it that obvious?"

"Only when he gets within fifty feet of you." Janet reached across the table to give Brigitte's hand a squeeze. "It must be awkward for you having the whole family around you while you're getting to know someone."

Brigitte sighed like a balloon deflating. "It never has been before. Oh, Janet, it's so complicated. I fell for him like logs rolling down a mountainside and he's so—" She searched for a word. "Weird!"

"Weird?"

The perplexed expression on her sister-in-law's face—so reflective of her own confusion—provoked a groan from Brigitte. "Damn!"

Janet's concern turned into alarm. "Brigitte, if he's hurt you—"

Brigitte frowned impatiently. "It's nothing like *that*. I said weird, not perverted."

"That's a relief. So what's so weird about him?"

Brigitte poured out the entire story, and concluded, "So you see, it's like he's two people, and the man I was falling in love with disappeared and some arrogant jerk who hates me took his place. Only he looks the same, and I still—"

"I don't believe it!"

"You've seen the way he's been acting . . . the mixed messages."

"I'm not talking about C. H. Battle!" Janet said. "I'm talking about you. It's quite a shock seeing you knocked off center."

"A shock?"

"When I married Stephen and moved here, I thought you were probably the most self-confident woman I'd ever met."

"Me?"

"Yes, you. You're beautiful, you're smart, you're full of energy, you're great at your job, you're always surrounded by admiring men." She smiled slyly. "I wasn't sure it was going to be easy to like you. But, of course, you're also *nice*, so it would have been impossible not to like you, even if you hadn't been Stephen's sister."

"And now you can't believe a woman like *me* is having man problems?"

"It's a stretch," Janet admitted. "But it's obvious this whole thing has you thrown."

"So the perfect woman has a heart like anyone else," Brigitte retorted sarcastically. "Call a press conference!"

"I didn't mean it that way," Janet said. "If you'd heard what I was trying to say, it was that I never expected to feel like you were a *sister*. But I do, and I'm concerned for you."

Brigitte exhaled a sigh. "I wondered, you know, why you seemed . . . reserved around me."

"You were so together, you scared the hell out of me. Oh, Brigitte, Charlie strikes me as being kind of shy. Maybe a woman like you . . . Maybe you scare the hell out of *him*, too."

"Charlie afraid?" Brigitte asked incredulously. "The man is a mountain. He could level me with a single blow."

"He wouldn't be afraid to fight with you, Brigitte. It's *loving* you that would scare him."

"Why?"

"Good grief, Brigitte. Look at the Dumont mystique. Your father was an international playboy, your parents' love story is legendary, and Stephen wasn't exactly a low-profile bachelor. You've been surrounded by dynamic men, romance and glamour all your life. Could you blame him for being intimidated?"

Brigitte gave the idea some thought, allowing herself a moment's hope before self-preservation triumphed over rosy optimism. "Then again," she said dismally, "he may be involved with someone else and doesn't want to get involved any further with me. He may have decided that he doesn't like the way I comb my hair or something. He may wonder what he ever saw in me."

"It sounds to me as though you need to ask the good detective a few questions."

"I tried," Brigitte said. "I opened my mouth to ask, but . . ."

"What happened?"

"He gave me that *stare* and I chickened out. I think I was afraid of what I might find out."

"Could he tell you anything—*anything*—that would make you more miserable than you are right now?"

"He could have a terminal disease or something."

"You've got to find out."

"You know something, Janet? It was quite a shock when Stephen brought home a wife, but you were so good for him that I had to forgive you for stealing my big brother away from me." She smiled. "Now I'm glad that I did, because obviously you're good for me, too."

"I feel as though we're almost real sisters," Janet said.

"What's this 'almost' business?" Brigitte demanded, grinning.

The door burst open at that moment, and Stephen and Charlie came marching in. "Oh, good," Stephen said, spying his wife and his sister. "You're both here. The way you two disappeared, I was afraid we might have to beep you. Charlie wants to talk about the mystery."

"I thought we weren't doing anything new until tomorrow morning," Janet said wearily. "Aren't the teams supposed to meet on their own tonight after the auction and write out what they think happened?"

"We need to toss out one more shocker to keep things popping," Charlie explained. He pinned Brigitte with a pointed look. "It's time for Babycakes to do her thing."

Brigitte responded with an exaggerated groan.

"You probably need to brief Brigitte," Janet said. "Stephen and I will give you some space."

She was practically pushing Stephen in the direction of the bedroom. Brigitte caught her eye and grinned wryly at her obvious attempt to leave them alone.

"Charlie wants to talk to us, too, Janet," Stephen told her, refusing to be railroaded out of the room.

"That's right," Charlie said. "What Babycakes reveals will affect your characters, too." His gaze was leveled on Brigitte's face. "If she's convincing enough."

"She was pretty convincing with that yardstick line," Stephen pointed out.

"Brigitte always plays her part well, don't you, Brigitte?" Charlie declared, with stinging sarcasm.

"I do my best," Brigitte retorted.

"So," said Janet, "can I get you guys something to drink?"

*A shot of hemlock, perhaps,* Brigitte thought unkindly.

Both men shook their heads. "We just came from the bar," Stephen said. "Although we could hardly bend our elbows with the sleuths hovering around, eavesdropping while Charlie pressured me about the accident with my hand." He chortled, then looked at Charlie. "Where did you get the idea Janet might have hit me with a rolling pin?"

Janet feigned surprise. "Those amateur detectives and their wild theories! So . . . what's on the agenda for the dinner hour?"

"I'm going to question Babycakes about her lingerie," Charlie replied, making it sound as appealing as a visit to a hospital emergency room.

"Also known as a pair of red lace panties," Brigitte speculated.

"Oh, good. They've been asking you about them," Charlie said. "I was hoping they would."

"Why don't you just tell me what I'm supposed to do, so we can go downstairs and get it done," Brigitte suggested.

Charlie told her.

"Is that all?" she asked sarcastically.

Charlie returned her hostile stare, then grinned devilishly. "Then you kiss me."

## 10

"BABYCAKES."

"Detective Fuzz."

Brigitte was certain she heard the thunk of fifty dessertspoons hitting the tables as the weekenders abandoned Gérard's Bloodred Cherry Mousse in order to turn their undivided attention to the vignette being acted out on the stage. Normally she thrived on a rapt audience, but this was one performance she would gladly have skipped. Charlie had coached her thoroughly on the clues he wanted to feed to the guests along with dessert.

Ordinarily, the scenario would have appealed to her quirky sense of fun. But there was nothing ordinary about the circumstances between her and the man sharing the stage with her. If she'd hoped to clear the air between them, she'd abandoned that hope in the face of his blatant hostility. The tension between them was thick enough to slice up and serve on a plate, and the subject matter of this little vignette was destined to drive that tension to new heights. Nerves over this performance had prevented her from enjoying the dinner. Now she just hoped she could make it through without cracking under the strain.

Charlie sounded quite authoritarian as he stepped into the Fantasy Fuzz character. "I need to ask you a few questions about something that was found at the scene of the crime."

Brigitte forced herself to chuck Charlie under the chin with her forefinger. "You don't mean those unmentionables everyone's been whispering about, do you, Detective Fuzz?"

"Are they yours, Babycakes?"

Brigitte slithered against his chest and cradled his cheek with her fingertips. "I never discuss unmentionables in public."

"They're red, Babycakes. Red lace bikinis."

"How naughty!" Brigitte said.

"I bet you look good in red."

"I look better in nothing at all," she purred.

Charlie swallowed. Fantasy Fuzz handled Babycakes with stoic aplomb. But he was flesh and blood, and the body Brigitte Dumont was rubbing against him was too real, too soft and far too voluptuous for his comfort.

"You're avoiding the issue, Babycakes."

"Oh, Fantasy, I make it a habit to avoid—" Brigitte blew in his ear "—issues. They're usually so-o-o depressing."

"You can't avoid these!" Charlie exclaimed, snatching a pair of panties from his pocket and holding them up in the air.

Brigitte stared at the red panties as though they were a poisonous viper. The blood drained from her face. She sought out Stephen and Janet in the crowd, and stared at them, until Charlie demanded, "What's the verdict, Babycakes? These yours or not?"

Brigitte looked stunned. "You found these in Vincent's bed?"

"Right between the sheets."

Brigitte looked at Stephen and Janet again, then turned back to Fantasy. "Guilty," she said, reaching for the panties.

"Not so fast, Babycakes," Charlie warned, holding them just out of her reach. His gaze cut to her hips. "I'm not sure these are your size."

"Of course, they are. You wouldn't expect to find another woman's unmentionables in my fiancé's bed, would you?"

"You don't happen to remember where you bought them, do you, Babycakes?"

"Where I buy all my unmentionables," she replied, putting her hand on the ball of his shoulder and propping her chin on it and batting her eyelashes at him. "At this adorable little lingerie boutique called Sin's Skins." She uttered the words like a dirty proposition.

Charlie had to wait for the applause to subside before continuing, which was just as well, because he was finding it difficult to concentrate on being Fantasy Fuzz. "Sin's Skins. That's very interesting. Tell me, Babycakes, do they carry a lot of maternity underwear?"

Babycakes lost her poise, but quickly regained it. "Maternity underwear? In red lace? Don't be silly, Detective."

"Read the label, Babycakes," he directed, showing her the satin tag in the side seam. "La Sexy Mama. A very expensive line of maternity lingerie made for women who don't think they have to lose their sexual appeal when they're pregnant."

"I never read the labels. I just see how sheer the lace is."

"This particular style is sold only as part of a packaged set that includes these bikini panties and a special support bra."

"Obviously the owner of Sin's Skins bought the set and sold the pieces separately."

"That might be true . . . if these were yours."

"Of course, they're mine."

"I don't think so, Babycakes."

"Why would I say they were if they weren't?"

"You could be embarrassed to admit that your fiancé was seeing another woman."

Brigitte draped herself against Charlie. "You're just full of theories, aren't you, Detective?"

"Or you could be covering for someone?"

She cocked her head at a jaunty angle. "What could I possibly cover with anything that sheer? Besides, why would I cover for someone who was fooling around with my fiancé?"

"Maybe because you think you're protecting someone you love. Someone you suspect of murder."

"I'm not the noble type."

"What type are you?"

"I'm the warm, squeezable type," she said. "I'm surprised you didn't notice, with your eye for detail."

"I noticed, Babycakes." He pulled her into his arms, and the audience clapped.

Brigitte looked up at him. "Did you notice my kissable lips?"

"Does this answer your question?" he asked. He'd vowed to remain in character, impassive to Brigitte, but the instant his mouth touched hers he accepted the futility of that vow. He couldn't remain indifferent to a woman whose very presence sent his senses reeling. For two days he'd been watching her, aware of her beauty, captivated by the grace in the way she moved, enchanted by her face and her form.

Each draw of breath brought him the scent of her: elusive, feminine, potent. Her body teased his with its sweet warmth. He involuntarily pulled her closer to him and she came all too willingly.

How could he have been foolish enough to think he could go through the motions of kissing her without getting pulled into the inferno of wanting she ignited in him? He felt her lips swell, soften and part, the acquiescence of surrender in her muscles as she relaxed and molded herself against him.

He kissed her. It was supposed to be a dramatic display—Fantasy Fuzz and Babycakes in mid-investigation. Instead, it was violent with frustrated passion.

Brigitte had planned on going through the motions, pleasing the audience. The kiss was supposed to be a stage kiss, part of the show, a crowd pleaser. She was Babycakes, the nubile suspect, trying to distract diligent Detective Fuzz. The kiss was supposed to be meaningless to her except for its distractive effects on Fuzz—only it *wasn't* meaningless to Brigitte Dumont.

If she were reacting normally, she would be enjoying herself, enjoying the spotlight, having fun with the cartoon character she was playing. But she wasn't reacting normally. She'd stopped reacting normally the moment C. H. Battle had first turned that hungry gaze on her, then won her over with his charm.

She was confused by the turmoil he'd brought to her ordered world. And there had been no getting to know each other, no testing of their feelings. There had been only that sudden plunge into tumultuous attraction. She'd fallen in love with him without knowing him at all. His change of attitude still nagged like a thorn lodged under her skin. She desperately wanted to remain unmoved by him, unresponsive to his virile body; yet her pulse raced when he touched her, and her breath caught at the prospect of his kiss.

She resented the power he had to make her ache for him in spite of his coldness and wanted to strike out at him for making her vulnerable to him; yet, as his mouth lowered to hers, she could do nothing but surrender to the spell of being in his arms.

Her acquiescence was complete the moment he touched her. His strength and size and warmth enveloped her. His lips seduced her. She wrapped her arms around his neck, aligning her body with his. She was scarcely aware when he lifted her feet off the floor, even less aware when the audience went wild with appreciative applause. She was only conscious of the man holding her and the feelings he aroused in her. Lost in sensation, she didn't notice the bright whiteness of the spotlight pouring down on them.

Charlie slowly lowered her to the floor, lifting his mouth from hers only after her feet were firmly planted on the stage. He loosened his embrace but still held her. She wasn't sure she could have stood without his support, and wondered if he sensed that.

From somewhere in the back of her mind, a message emerged, urgent, nagging. *Say the line, Brigitte. Say the line.* But it took her a few seconds too long to remember what line she was supposed to say and force it through her tightened throat. The breathless quality of her voice was real as she rasped, "Oh, Fantasy."

The spotlight popped off, leaving the room in total darkness except for the lighted exit markers above the doors. Brigitte was suddenly aware of where she was, of the audience still applauding what they believed to be a magnificent performance—and *acutely aware* of what Charlie had made her feel.

Embarrassed, Brigitte fled. She was so familiar with the room that she was able to reach the most convenient door without breaking her neck in the darkness. She dashed through the kitchen to the service hall, where she took the back elevator to her private suite.

Charlie was left feeling as if Brigitte had performed a magical disappearing act. One second she was in his arms; the next, she was gone. And he'd never felt any loss more keenly in his life.

Stephen and Janet were waiting for him when he found the presence of mind to leave the bandstand. The house lights were back on, and the tables were abuzz with discussion of the latest developments in the mystery.

"I want to talk to you, Battle," Stephen said, grabbing Charlie's elbow and hustling him through the hovering sleuths who hoped to overhear some significant exchange. Janet scurried after them, stopping at the door to cut off those persistent enough to follow them with assurances that she and Stephen would return shortly.

She joined Charlie and Stephen, and gave Stephen a wry smile. "One of the attorneys thinks you're confessing and turning yourself in. He wanted to represent you."

"That doesn't matter now," Stephen said, scowling at Charlie. "If you weren't a special guest of the hotel and if those people in the dining room hadn't paid through the nose to see you in action, I'd bounce your behind right out of here."

Charlie was thoroughly bewildered. "What's the problem?"

"Don't play dumb, Battle. The issue is my sister."

"Brigitte?" Charlie's suspicions were confirmed. Brigitte's hasty exit *had* been significant and, worse, what should have remained a private matter between the two of them had become public. He had a sick feeling deep in his gut that he'd bungled everything beyond redemption. He felt about two inches tall.

"I don't know what's going on between the two of you, but I'm not blind. You kept firing off potshots upstairs, and she was wound up tight enough to bounce quarters off. I haven't said anything because I figure she's a big girl and can take care of herself. But I've never seen her tuck tail and run the way she just ran out of this room. So, whatever's going on—"

"Stephen." Janet said it softly yet firmly. Stephen grudgingly shifted his gaze from Charlie's face to hers. "Someone has to check on Brigitte," she insisted.

"Go on," Stephen said. "I'll be up later."

"I told the guests we'd be out to talk to them. Let Charlie go."

"Him? He's the reason she—"

Janet stayed him with her hand on his forearm. "That's why he has to go." She looked at Charlie. "That is, if he wants to straighten things out."

Charlie gave her a grateful nod. "I'd like to talk to her."

Stephen scowled, but Janet gave Charlie directions to Brigitte's suite.

"You hurt her—" Stephen warned.

"I won't," Charlie assured him. *Not intentionally.* At the moment, he wouldn't have given anyone odds that he wouldn't bungle things further, but he was desperate for a chance to talk to Brigitte. Her sister-in-law had handed him that chance, and he was going for it.

As he started up the hallway, he overheard Stephen express his doubts about the situation and heard Janet reply, "Just trust me, okay?"

Brigitte didn't say anything when she opened the door to her suite, just stared at him warily. He felt a moment's panic over the prospect that she might not let him in, but she stepped back and closed the door behind him. She still wore the black dress she'd worn to dinner. He'd told her to wear something slinky and sexy, and she'd obliged. It clung to her hips, hugged her breasts, and left her shoulders almost bare.

She'd taken off her shoes, and was padding about in her stocking feet. He was relieved to see that although she looked unhappy, she didn't appear to have been crying. After stopping in the middle of the room to give him a sharp look, she walked to the sofa and settled into a corner of it, curling up with her legs tucked under. Her knees strained whitely against her black stockings and her polished toenails showed bright pink through the sheer toes.

After a tense stretch of silence, Charlie sat down in a wing chair facing the sofa and just looked at her. Maybe it was the wounded expression in her eyes. Maybe it was the fact that she looked small and vulnerable. Charlie just knew that he felt big and clumsy, and as mean as a playground bully stealing cookies from lunch boxes.

"I just want to know why," she said with a quiet, deadly calm.

"Why?"

He watched her throat convulse as she swallowed, saw her close her eyes as if she fought for the right words, for the strength to say them. "I'm no kid, Charlie. I've met lots of men here at the chalet. I flirt a lot, but I'm careful about who I let close to me. I'm not part of the 'amenities.'"

She studied her hands while regrouping her thoughts. Charlie wanted to help her out but didn't know how, so he waited in futile silence, still feeling mean, though wishing he could comfort her. He wondered what she'd do if he moved on to the sofa and wrapped his arms around her, and was afraid to try, for fear of further alienating her. Even Fuzz would be at a loss in this situation, he thought grimly.

"Sometimes I meet men I'd like to know longer than the week or two weeks they stay here. Sometimes they call or write. Sometimes they even come back." Her smile was sad and, somehow, courageous. "Sometimes they promise to call or come back, then don't."

She paused again. "The point is, Charlie, some of them didn't live up to their promises, but that's all. They just . . . didn't live up to their promises. But I can't think of a single time, in my whole life, that a man has deliberately hurt me the way you have."

*Deliberately hurt her?* Charlie was stunned at the accusation. Stunned, and guilty. He *had* wanted to hurt her, because he'd felt betrayed. He just hadn't realized he *could* hurt her so; that he had that much power over her. "Brigitte—"

"I can see how maybe things just got a little . . . out of perspective. Maybe the time we spent together didn't seem so special to you after you got home."

"It *was* special," Charlie said stoically.

"I can see how you might have second thoughts or regrets—especially about leaving me the note. But why'd you send me another one? Did you get some kind of thrill out of leading me on and then treating me like yesterday's garbage?"

"I was hurt!" Charlie replied.

"Hurt? You?"

"I thought what happened between us was . . . It wasn't something that happened to me every day. I could hardly wait to see you again. And then I picked up *Contemporary Canada* and read all about us."

"*Contemporary Canada?* You mean Donna's article?"

"The one where you gave our kiss a Richter-scale rating."

"That's what you've been so bent out of shape about? That's why you've been treating me like dirt under your feet? Because of that stupid article?"

"It wasn't stupid to me. You Dumonts may be used to seeing your personal life detailed in print, but I'm not. I confided in you, because . . . hell, because I let you—your face and your body and the way you smell—get to me. And then . . . You're crying."

"You're damned right, I'm crying!" Brigitte retorted, impatiently smearing a tear across her cheek with the back of her hand. "But don't you for one second think I'm crying because I'm hurt. This is pure rage, Mr. C. H. Battle!"

"You're mad at me?"

"How dare you?" she exclaimed, leaping to her feet to glare down at him. "How dare you just *assume* that I went to Donna and poured my heart out to her for publication. How dare you treat me as though I was some sort of traitor selling state secrets!"

Charlie stood and, towering over her, accused her. "I've never told anyone else that I didn't know how to dance."

"Well, you didn't tell me it was a deep, dark secret."

"You rated our kiss like a . . . a new song on the radio."

"You nincompoop! I didn't rate anything. Donna said that the kiss in front of the camera looked like at least a seven on the Richter and I sort of . . . idly agreed. Did you want me to lie? Most men would be flattered to have their effect on women compared to a natural disaster!"

"I'm not most men. I'm a very private man."

"You're also a celebrity. You were the subject of that article, not me."

"What happened between us was private. You talked to a reporter about it."

"I didn't talk to her about what happened between us when we were alone. She said she'd found out you were a social recluse and I said that you didn't know how to dance. And I don't see how you can be so sanctimonious about privacy when you're the one who turned that kiss in front of the camera into an earth-shattering spectacle."

"I just kissed you."

"That's like saying King Kong was just a monkey."

"You kissed me back!"

"Ex-cuu-se me!"

They fell silent. Brigitte sat down on the couch again, and stared at the magazine on the end table, at her hands, at the wall—anywhere except at Charlie, who was actively staring out the window.

Brigitte choked back a sob. "You know what really hurts, Charlie? It's that you seem to think that because my name is Dumont, I'm incapable of feeling anything genuine. I should have seen it coming when you accused me of 'turning it on and off.' It's as though you assumed I had to pretend *all* the time because I was incapable of honest reaction."

Charlie ventured a glance at her, which confirmed his suspicions that she was crying again. "It was nothing like that."

"It's exactly like that." She brushed away tears with her fingertips. "I got a dose of it from my sister-in-law this very day. She thought I was so together and so confident, that I'd never let a man hurt me. As though I had some kind of insulation that prevents me from caring that much."

"I never meant—"

She raised her tearstained face to look at him. The sight of it was an accusation Charlie couldn't deny he deserved.

"You were ready enough to believe I could be shallow enough to run to Donna and tell her everything that happened between us. Did you think I wanted her to put it in the magazine? Did you think I would get some perverted thrill out of everyone in Canada knowing that we'd danced and kissed in the fitness room? Did you think I was so shallow and insecure that I had some crazy idea that they'd think I was sexy because the great C. H. Battle found me attractive?"

"I didn't think anything like that. I was... It was so new to me, Brigitte. I was scared to trust—"

"Scared to trust *me*? Because I'm a Dumont?"

"I was getting in over my head. It was happening so fast, and it was so overwhelming. I felt as though I'd fallen over a cliff."

"You weren't the only one falling!"

Charlie felt as though he were falling again, tumbling hopelessly into a bottomless pit of guilt from which there would be no rescue or recovery. "I'm sorry," he said, feeling the emptiness and futility of his words. "I was scared, Brigitte. You got to me, and then I saw the article."

She just sat there, crying silently and looking stricken. Charlie would have ripped his heart out if he'd thought it would make her feel any better. He eased down on the opposite end of the sofa, careful not to touch her for fear it would make things worse, though he couldn't imagine things any worse. They were both miserable, and he hadn't the slightest idea how to help alleviate that misery.

Some perverse streak of hope that refused to die compelled him to try again. One more time. He was capable of nothing except candor. "I don't know anything about women, Brigitte. I don't have the experience most men have. I didn't mean to hurt you. I was just scared of the way you made me feel."

She continued to sob, and he pleaded. "Please don't cry anymore, Brigitte."

She sniffed. "You really don't know anything at all about women, do you?"

He shook his head. The expression in his eyes was that of a man in a desperate state.

"The last thing a woman wants when she's crying is for a man to ask her not to cry anymore."

Charlie threw up his hands in a gesture of helplessness.

"Oh, Charlie," she said, shaking her head. "Haven't you ever heard of kissing it to make it better?"

# 11

BRIGITTE WAS LIFTED into his arms almost before she had a chance to register that he'd moved. He held her so close she could scarcely breathe, while his lips moved greedily from her mouth to her cheeks to her neck, whispering endearments amid impatient kisses.

Relief oozed through her. She'd thought she'd never feel these arms around her again; she'd been terrified she'd never hear sweet words whispered in that deep voice. Wounded emotions healed as she clung to him. Lingering doubts evaporated as she responded to his kisses with her own urgent ardor. She was in love.

Charlie wanted to absorb the hurt he'd caused her. He couldn't hug her tightly enough to assure himself that she was actually there, next to him. He tasted the salt of her tears, reveled in the sweet softness of her skin under his lips and the pressure of her hands on his back.

"I couldn't quit thinking of you," he rasped into her ear. "I haven't been able to work. My concentration's shot. My characters kept looking like you."

He fused his mouth over hers, hungrily claiming, affirming. She felt soft and sensual and sexy—all the things in a woman that make a man feel strong and special. He was filled with passion and tenderness, and so overwhelmed by the need to soothe her that he dragged his mouth from hers to say, "I'm sorry I hurt you. I was wrong to doubt you. I see that so clearly now...."

She shushed him by pressing her fingertips over his lips. "You've said enough, Charlie."

Charlie had never been eloquent except in his art, but now he desperately searched for the words to persuade her of his sincerity.

She grabbed the fronts of his jacket and yanked them forward, forcing his face down as she thrust her own face up, nose to nose with him. "You've said everything that needs saying. It's time for action, not talk."

He stared at her, wanting her so fiercely he thought his desire for her must surely be visible, like an aura of light.

"I'm looking at you that way again, Charlie," she said impatiently.

Charlie was paralyzed by the intensity of her words, and fearful of doing anything to shatter the spell.

She released his jacket fronts slowly, giving him a look that could give a man erotic dreams. Then she turned her back to him and looked over her shoulder to smile a smile that exuded sensual promise. "Unzip my dress, Charlie."

His fingers trembled, but the delay only heightened the anticipation. Finally her dress gaped open, and he stared at her smooth back, too awestruck by the perfection of her body to dare to touch it.

After an eternity of seconds, Brigitte took several tentative steps away from him, then paused to look back over her shoulder, silently inviting him to follow. She led him into the bedroom and stopped near the bed. She could hear his breathing as he stood behind her, and somehow felt the heat of his hungry gaze on her flesh almost as poignantly as she would have felt a physical touch. Her mouth dry, she waited.

Charlie stared at her. Her back was completely bare down to the waistband of her panty hose, and below, hugged by sheer black nylon, the feminine swell of her hips curved, inviting his touch. Her skin glowed pale in contrast to the black dress framing it. He knew without touching that it would be as soft as velvet.

"I want to touch every inch of you."

"I'll be disappointed if you don't," she said huskily.

Charlie raised his fingertips and rested them lightly on her shoulder blades. He'd never known how stimulating sound could be until he heard the combination of gasp and sigh that rose in Brigitte's throat as she arched her neck back.

She turned. Her dress had slipped down, leaving her shoulders intimately bare. Her cheeks were flushed a beguiling scarlet, and her lips were slightly swollen from his kisses. A man had no right to see a woman in such a state if he wasn't willing to love her, Charlie thought. He *was* willing, and more than ready to take on the responsibility.

She lifted her hands to the front of his shirt and he watched, mesmerized, as she unbuttoned it. When she brushed the sides apart and leaned forward, he tensed in anticipation. She nestled her cheek against his chest and sighed.

The sweetness of having her there as she wrapped her arms around his waist was almost unbearable. Charlie put his hands on her shoulders, hoping she could discern from the reverence of his touch the tenderness he felt for her.

Brigitte had never felt so close to anyone as she did to Charlie while listening to the beat of his heart and feeling the rhythm of his breathing under her cheek. The richness of being there with him filled her to overflowing with a sense of well-being—a sense, almost, of having come home after a long absence.

She shoved his shirt back, pushing the jacket aside at the same time. Charlie cooperated with a shrug of his shoulders that sent both garments to the floor. He didn't realize she was wriggling out of her dress until her breasts pressed against his ribs, sending a shock of desire burning through him. He looked down to discover her face tilted up, inviting his kiss. He obliged her gently, but thoroughly.

She was his. The frankness of her response, with its lack of pretense or defense, was testament to her trust in him. He had hurt her deeply, yet she obviously held nothing back, erected no barrier to protect herself. That she should make herself so vulnerable to him touched his heart, his soul. He belonged to her as completely as she belonged to him.

Charlie was only vaguely aware of her wedging her hands between their bodies to open the waistband of his pants until the pressure of her hand sliding the zipper along the length of his erection drew an involuntary gasp from his lungs. His entire body tensed as he waited for her touch, but she surprised him again by following his waistband around to his back and pushing her hands below the loosened fabric to knead his buttocks, and pull him more tightly against her.

Charlie growled a feral growl of need and his arousal strained against the knot of his underwear. As if in response, Brigitte released his trousers and briefs. They slid down his legs easily but lodged around his ankles. Impatient to step out of them, Charlie had to get his shoes off first. When at last he'd kicked everything aside, he returned his full attention to Brigitte.

She had sat down on the edge of the bed and was guiding her stockings down over her calves. Charlie's eyes were drawn to her breasts, which bobbed enticingly as she moved. Following the direction of his gaze, she smiled at him knowingly, then continued her task with deliberate slowness until she'd freed her stockings and tossed them aside with a flamboyant flick of her wrist and a throaty laugh.

A moment of seriousness followed. Brigitte's frivolous laughter faded into an enigmatic smile as she admired him, and Charlie suddenly felt self-conscious standing there, aroused and exposed. But when Brigitte stood, with only a strip of beige satin and lace shielding her from his view and made no effort to hide herself further, his embarrassment was forgotten as he feasted on the sight of her.

Stepping close to him, she raised her hands to cradle his face. "I love you, you know."

She said the words tentatively, as though testing them. The weight of meaning in them stunned Charlie. It was obvious that they didn't roll off her tongue with the familiarity of practice. He was struck by the awesome responsibility of being loved by a woman, not certain he was ready for it in one fell swoop. Then Brigitte slipped her arms around his neck and hugged him. He sought her mouth with his and, finding it, conquered it while stroking her body with his hands. Her breasts fit perfectly against his palms.

Brigitte wriggled restlessly against him and made whimpering sounds in her throat as he kissed her, which aroused him to the edge of madness.

He tore his mouth away from hers to look into her eyes, and found proof of her love. Scooping her up, he carried her to the bed and tumbled onto the softness with her.

Immediately Brigitte rolled on top of him and began to cover him with urgent kisses, exploring his body with her mouth and hands. She seemed insatiable, and her ardor made him hungrier for her.

He was too distracted by the pressure of her body on his to realize that she was fumbling with the pillow beneath his head, until she pulled a foil pouch from inside the pillowcase. Her voice was breathless. "I put this here yesterday morning." The expression on her face softened as she looked down at him. "I left it there. I didn't have the heart to give up on us."

Affected by her sentiment and incapable of words, Charlie guided her face to his for a gentle kiss he hoped would be as eloquent. He moaned when she caressed his erection, which hardened even more under her touch.

With loving sweeps of her fingertips she put the sheath in place, then rose to kneel beside him.

He looked up at her, past her flat midriff and the alluring swell of her breasts to her face, which was framed by the wild halo of her hair. Her eyes spoke of adoration and love; her swollen lips and flushed cheeks, of passion. She lifted her fingertips to her lips, then lowered them to Charlie's. Never taking her gaze from his face, she looped her thumbs under the elastic of her panties and shoved them past her hips. They caught at her knees and, smiling, she lay down next to Charlie and finished removing them, then rolled on her side and opened her arms to him beseechingly.

He came over her, spreading one thigh across hers while he buried his face between her breasts. He sighed as she kneaded his back muscles with urgent longing. He chafed her breasts with his palms, then teased their taut peaks with his tongue, thrilling at the guttural sounds with which she responded.

Brigitte thrust her lower body against him, communicating her readiness and need. She opened to him, and sighed languidly when his body linked with hers. She was an uninhibited lover—both greedy and generous. Locking her legs around him, she pressed hot kisses on his neck, driving him to peaks of pleasure more intense than he'd ever imagined, and to a plateau of tenderness he'd never known he could attain.

Charlie wanted to consume her and he wanted to protect her. Most of all, he wanted to give to her as freely as she gave to him. He tried to pace their lovemaking, but his own raging desire made a mockery of his intentions as she strained against him in a frenzied search for fulfillment. He gave himself up to sensation as the excitement between them mounted.

Brigitte cried out, tensing against him with a powerful thrust. She clung to him with shocking strength, as though her very life depended on remaining close to him. Charlie held her, feeling the waves inside her as she climaxed, then succumbed to his own climax. The force of it racked him from head to toe. He shuddered then collapsed over her.

He lay there, his mind as paralyzed as his body was drained, until he'd recovered enough to register that a gentle hand was brushing his hair from his forehead. Pushing up onto his elbows, he looked down at Brigitte in alarm. "Did I hurt you?"

She laughed softly at his stricken expression. "You did many things to me, but hurting was not one of them."

He rolled aside. "I'm too heavy."

"You're incredible."

"I, uh, need to—" Charlie said, glad of the excuse the condom gave him to flee into the bathroom temporarily so he could regain some perspective. After what they'd just experienced, he wasn't quite ready to deal with accolades.

When he returned, she was lying on her side, propped on one elbow, wearing her bikini underpants and Charlie's Fantasy Fuzz bombardier jacket. He sat down on the edge of the bed. "Are you all right?"

Brigitte rolled onto her back, stretched, and sighed. "Oh, Fantasy."

Charlie attempted not to notice how far apart the fronts of the jacket had drifted. "It was Charlie Battle in bed with you. Fantasy Fuzz is just a doodle on paper."

Alarmed by the harshness in his voice, she sat up again. "I was only teasing."

"I wouldn't want you confused."

She moved next to him on the edge of the bed. Then she lifted her hands to cradle his face, making it impossible for him to ignore what the open jacket couldn't hide.

"Why is it I feel I don't have your full attention?" she asked.

"You've got my full attention," he assured her.

"Parts of me do," she said wryly. Leaning forward, she crossed her forearms over his shoulder and propped her chin on them. "I'm not confused, Charlie. I don't even read *Fantasy Fuzz*."

Charlie weighed that information in the context of everything that had happened. He was confused—and he couldn't believe how good Brigitte's breasts felt, pressed against his biceps. "You meant it, didn't you?"

Brigitte saw the same expression she'd seen on his face when she'd told him she loved him. Snuggling a little closer, she sighed in his ear. "Yep, Charlie. I'm afraid so."

He mulled over her answer for several seconds before asking, "Why me?"

"I don't know," she purred, sliding her arms around his shoulders so that her breasts pressed against his chest. "You're a hunk, of course, but I've known lots of hunks, and none of them..." Idly running her fingers through his hair, she sighed again. "And it's not as though you sweet-talked me, is it?"

"I'm not much of a talker."

"You've got compensating qualities," Brigitte replied, guiding his head down to hers for a searing kiss.

Charlie ended the kiss before it turned into something more. He was already in over his head. "Brigitte..."

"You don't have to talk, Charlie," she said, sliding her leg over his so that she was straddling him. "You don't have to say a word."

As she settled against him and traced the shell of his ear with her tongue, he couldn't have uttered a word if his life had depended on it.

BRIGITTE BARELY HAD time to shower and put on fresh makeup before going downstairs for the auction. She walked into the dining room with few minutes to spare, and was instantly buttonholed by Janet, who turned a concerned face toward her. "Are you okay?"

"Yes," Brigitte replied, with a smug smile. "Better than okay."

"I knew it!" Janet exclaimed. "When Charlie came in strutting like a blue-ribbon rooster, I just *knew* it."

"He's here already?"

"Playing to the masses," Janet said, tilting her head toward the far side of the room, where a dozen of the guests were pumping him for new information about the murder mystery.

"How are things going down here?"

"Just the way we planned," Janet replied. "I've been reluctantly admitting to owning the red panties, and Stephen's been reluctantly confessing that he punched out Vincent in a fit of jealous rage—but steadfastly denying that he shot him. They seem ready to buy my story about the panties, but have some serious doubts about Stephen's innocence. They caught on to the suggestion that you lied about the panties, and they're all pretty convinced you did it to protect your brother. And speaking of protecting people, you should have seen your brother in action after you bolted out of here earlier."

"Stephen?"

Janet nodded. "He'd cornered Charlie and was—shall we say, demonstrating a bit of family loyalty?—when I managed to shift the focus from assault to negotiation."

"I had a feeling you had something to do with Charlie showing up on my doorstep."

"I just gave him directions to your suite. He was anxious to make amends."

"He made them!" Brigitte confirmed, and grinned mischievously. "So my big brother is intent on defending my virtue. We'd better hope he doesn't ask where the negotiations led."

"He's concerned about your happiness, Brigitte. Your virtue is your business. By the way, you're glowing."

"It shows?"

"Only to anyone with eyesight."

"*C'est la vie!*" Brigitte replied with a shrug. Then, looking over at Charlie, she said, "I think that, as special-events coordinator, I really should go rescue our guest of honor from those inquisitive sharks."

"Duty compels it," Janet agreed wryly. "See you later."

Brigitte elbowed her way through the crowd to Charlie. Their eyes met, and she gave him a seductive smile. "I like your jacket, Fantasy," Brigitte cooed, wrapping her left arm around him and splaying her right hand over his chest. "Do you ever loan it out?"

"No," Charlie said, hoping that the heat he felt rising in his face wasn't noticeable to the spectators of this impromptu performance. "But they're going to auction one just like it in a few minutes if you're interested, Babycakes."

Brigitte fluttered her eyelashes. "I may just bid."

"You into leather, Babycakes?"

"Only if I can wear it on bare skin," she countered, earning appreciative titters from the eavesdropping snoops.

Charlie decided it was going to be a long night for Fantasy Fuzz.

# 12

"WE ARE HERE," Fantasy Fuzz announced gravely the following morning, "to uncover the truth." The members of the Dumont family were gathered on the band platform, each looking appropriately apprehensive and indignant.

Detective Fuzz cast an accusing finger. "You, Babycakes!"

Brigitte had been leaning nonchalantly against the piano, and she pulled away from it, standing stiffly in front of her accuser. "Vincent was my fiancé!" she protested. "I wouldn't kill him."

"No, but you'd protect his killer. Especially if you felt the murder was justified."

"Don't be ridiculous! I loved him."

"And that made his infidelity even harder to deal with, didn't it, Babycakes? Particularly when you realized that his infidelity gave your brother a motive for murder."

Brigitte shot a panicked glance at Stephen. "No!"

Fuzz pressed on. "You lied about the underpants found in his bed."

"I bought those panties at Sin's Skins last month."

"Yes, but you didn't buy them for yourself. You bought them for your sister-in-law, who was feeling fat and clumsy with her pregnancy. A little morale booster for her and the brother you adore."

"That's not true."

"The clerk remembers selling them to you. She thought it was very sweet of you to do something so nice for your sister-in-law. You didn't expect those panties to show up in your fiancé's bed, did you? But when they did, you recognized them. Putting two and two together, you tried to protect your brother by claiming they were yours."

"Yes! I lied to protect Stephen," Brigitte admitted dramatically. "But not from murder charges. I lied because I didn't want him to know Janet had been there. I knew it would destroy him!" Turning to Stephen, she said, "I'm so sorry, Stephen."

"You could have skipped the lies, Babycakes. Stephen already knew his wife had been there." Fuzz turned his eagle eye on Janet. "Didn't he, Mrs. Dumont? That's why he went to Vincent Langton's room and came back with bruised knuckles, isn't it? He knew, because you told him."

"Yes! I told him!" Janet confessed tearfully. "I told him because I couldn't keep on living with the guilt. I didn't know—"

"You didn't know what?" Fuzz challenged. Janet buried her face in her hands and didn't answer. Fuzz moved along to Stephen. "She knew you'd be hurt and angry, but she didn't figure on your charging off like a white knight for revenge."

"He was blackmailing her!" Stephen charged. "She'd—" He looked at Janet with love in his eyes. "There'd been an indiscretion a few months ago. I had to go on a business trip, and Janet and I had had an argument before I left. Vincent—" He said the name as though it left a bad taste in his mouth. "Vincent was here, but Brigitte had some special event going on and had to work, so my 'friend' decided to comfort my wife."

Janet, somewhat recovered, dropped her hands into her lap and said, "It was a mistake, a horrible mistake. I'm not a drinker, but he kept mixing drinks, and before I knew it . . . I was sorry. All I could think of was how hurt Stephen would be if he ever found out."

"And you'd vowed he'd never find out," Fuzz added harshly. "How touching. But Vincent had other ideas."

"He wanted me to go to bed with him again," Janet said miserably. "He threatened to tell Stephen if I didn't. I begged and pleaded, but he just laughed. Finally I agreed, but at the last minute, I couldn't do it. Not sober. Not after the hell I'd been through over the guilt from the first time. I took off my clothes, but when he touched me, I couldn't stand it. I slapped him, and grabbed what clothing I could and threw it on and ran."

"And that's the story you heard from your hysterical wife, isn't it, Mr. Dumont?" Fuzz asked Stephen. "You were angry with her, but you were livid with Vincent. He'd cuckolded you, and he'd betrayed your sister, who was in love with him. Then he'd tried to extort more sex from your pregnant wife."

"I hit him!" Stephen confessed. "You're damned right, I hit him. I clipped him a good one on the jaw and then punched him in the gut as hard as I could. If you'd told me he died from internal injuries, I might believe I'd killed him. But he was alive when I left him, sitting up rubbing his jaw."

"Which brings us back to the original question," Fuzz continued. "Who put a bullet in Vincent Langton's heart? Was it Babycakes, here?"

Brigitte crossed her arms and scowled at him.

"You might have found out about Vincent's philandering and decided to extract some fatal revenge. Or it could have been the young Mrs. Dumont."

Janet's head snapped up. "Me?"

"He'd seduced you, tried to blackmail you. Maybe your husband wasn't in a forgiving mood, and you decided to vent your anger at Langton for destroying your marriage."

"I didn't even know about the gun!" Janet argued.

"That's right. But your husband knew about it. He might have decided that a clip on the jaw and a punch in the gut weren't adequate punishment."

"He couldn't have!" Janet said. "He came back to our suite with his knuckles all swollen and I fixed an ice pack for him. We talked for hours and then—" She blushed. "We made up. He was with me the entire evening."

"Again, back to the central issue," Fuzz said.

Jean-Pierre Dumont rose from his chair. "See here, Detective. For two days you've been questioning my family, exposing our dirty laundry in public!"

The weekend detectives, who'd been hanging on every word, laughed at the double entendre.

"If you have evidence against anyone, why don't you arrest them and get it over with. And if you don't, I'm afraid I'm going to have to ask you to leave the Chalet Dumont and stop harassing my family."

"Oh, there's evidence," Fuzz replied. "Take the murder weapon. It belonged to your wife."

"Are you suggesting that Marguerite—? If so you must be mad! My wife is the most genteel woman I've ever met. And I've met many women, Detective, as you surely know."

More laughter at the reference to Jean-Pierre's playboy days.

"Mrs. Dumont owned the gun, but all of your children knew of its existence. Let us suppose that your daughter, Claire Silvain, still carried a torch for Langton. He'd already flaunted his relationship with her younger sister in front of her, and he was starting on a new generation when he kissed her daughter. If she found out he'd seduced her brother's wife and was blackmailing her, it is not inconceivable she would plan to put an end to his philandering once and for all."

"That's ridiculous!" Claire said. "I had a crush on Vincent, but that was years ago, before I met Claude. I was thrilled when he and Brigitte announced their engagement. And the kiss under the mistletoe was perfectly harmless. We all saw him kiss her. Nicole was the only one who made a big deal of it."

"Maybe you knew you no longer carried a torch for Langton, but your husband wasn't so sure."

"Claude?" Claire asked incredulously.

"Jealousy does strange things to men."

"If all you have are wild theories, Detective, I'm afraid I must ask you to leave."

"You seem anxious for me to leave, Mr. Dumont."

Marguerite Dumont stood. "My husband does not mean to be ungracious, Detective Fuzz. This unpleasantness has us all on edge. Of course, you are welcome to stay until this case is resolved. But you're wasting your time trying to find a killer among my family. Obviously someone stole the gun and used it in an attempt to make it look as though someone in the family committed this crime."

"I don't believe so, Mrs. Dumont. The person who carried that gun to Vincent Langton's room and shot him in the heart had an accomplice. And it was a member of this family!"

*Accomplice?* The Dumonts and weekend sleuths reacted in unison.

"A very concerned accomplice. An accomplice who saw the killer put the gun in the ashtray, and later realized the importance of what she'd seen. An accomplice who then went back and took the gun to keep anyone else from finding it. That was a very courageous thing to do, Nicole. Who were you trying to protect?"

All eyes were turned on Nicole, who was shaking her head in denial. "I found it by accident!"

"That story doesn't wash anymore, Nicole. We took your fingerprints so we could identify them and discount them on the gun and the ashtray. But the lab didn't find any prints on the ashtray. None at all. There should have been lots of prints, Nicole. Any guest on the floor would have had access to it. The metal surface would have been a perfect medium for prints."

Nicole flicked her tongue over her lips to moisten them. "The killer must have wiped it off."

"Not before you touched it. Your prints should have been there. Even assuming the killer took the time to wipe it off—which is very unlikely—you had to touch it to take out the gun. But after you did that, you wiped it clean, because you knew who'd put it there, and you wanted to protect him, didn't you?"

"No!" Nicole cried hysterically.

"The killer wouldn't have left the gun in so obvious a place if he hadn't been under pressure to get rid of it in a hurry. He must have known it would be found, but he'd also known that there was a good chance it wouldn't be found until Housekeeping serviced that floor the next day. So for some reason—maybe he heard the elevator coming, or just wanted some extra time to decide what to do with the gun—he stashed the gun in the ashtray. He might have taken the time to wipe it off, but even if he'd wiped the ashtray as well, you would have put fresh prints on it when you opened it. Which leads us back to you, Nicole. You're a bright girl. You knew about fingerprints. You'd seen the killer put the gun in the ashtray, and when you heard about the murder, you went back to hide the gun, and you wiped the prints off the ashtray so no one would know he'd touched it. Who were you protecting, Nicole?"

"Nobody!" Nicole exclaimed. "I just found the gun!"

"She did," Jennifer said. "She told me all about it."

"She knew who the murderer was," continued Fuzz, "and she knew she had to protect him. She couldn't tell anyone, not even you. After all, you spilled the beans about the gun. She must have known you couldn't keep a secret like the identity of the killer."

"It's not true!" Nicole insisted. "I didn't see him! I didn't see anybody. I just saw the ashtray."

"You're a very brave and very loyal girl, Nicole. You must love the killer very much to want to protect him, to lie for him."

"I'm not lying! I'm not—"

"You are!" Fuzz insisted. "You wiped off the ashtray and you wiped off the gun."

"No. No, no, no, no!"

"Detective Fuzz!" Jean-Pierre Dumont chided indignantly. "I must protest your treatment of this child. My granddaughter is upset enough by Vincent Langton's death. I'll not have you browbeating her. She is not in the habit of lying."

"No." Fantasy turned a firm but sympathetic eye on Nicole, then shifted his attention back to Jean-Pierre. "She's not in the habit of lying. But these are extraordinary circumstances, are they not? It's not every day that an infatuated young lady learns that her jovial Uncle Vin has been killed."

Nicole gasped, and Jean-Pierre said, "Detective, please, have some sensitivity to the child's emotional state."

"*And*, it's not every day that a young lady realizes that her beloved grandfather is guilty of murder, and feels compelled to protect him."

Jean-Pierre straightened and thrust his chin in the air.

"He was destroying your family, wasn't he, Mr. Dumont? He'd dallied with the affections of both your daughters. He was flirting with your granddaughter and he was threatening your son's marriage. That was his final mistake, wasn't it, Dumont? You have two granddaughters."

"I love my granddaughters more than life itself," Jean-Pierre declared.

"But they're Silvains, not Dumonts. And even if they were Dumonts, they would likely take their husbands' names. The child Janet is carrying could be a son. A Dumont heir to carry on the name you brought to prominence. If Vincent had succeeded in breaking up her marriage to Stephen, she would have been forced to leave, taking the child with her. And if the child turned out to be a girl, with no marriage there would have been no other chances for a male heir. And the odds of Stephen finding another wife and producing a son in your lifetime were slim."

"You make me sound like a European monarch, obsessed by the desire for a male issue. Is it so wrong to want to see the Dumont name live on after I'm gone? Is it so wrong to want to protect my family? I saw Janet leave his room with tearstains on her cheeks. I followed her and stood in the hallway outside their suite and heard the sounds of her sobs. Then Stephen came charging out and I followed him to Vincent's room. I heard the sounds of a fight, and saw Stephen leave. I went to Vincent and asked him to leave my family alone. I asked him to break his engagement to Brigitte and never return to the chalet, but he would not listen to reason. He talked about having Stephen arrested for assault, and creating a scandal. He said he would convince Brigitte to leave with him because he had complete influence over her. I could not let him tear my family apart, Detective. *Oui*, I murdered Vincent Langton, and I would do it again."

"Jean-Pierre!" Marguerite exclaimed, leaping from her chair to fling her arms around him. "Don't say any more. We'll get a lawyer—"

Ignoring her pleas, Jean-Pierre turned to Nicole. "I did not mean to involve you in this, *ma petite*." He raised his gaze to Fuzz. "I have confessed. There is no need to involve her any further. She is only a child."

"A very precocious child," Fuzz remarked. "She came to visit Uncle Vin alone. As she approached the door, it opened and you came out, so she had to duck inside a doorway to keep from being seen. Then she saw you panic and hide the gun."

"The elevator had stopped on the floor above, so I knew there would be a passenger," Jean-Pierre said.

"So Nicole waited for you to leave, ran to Vincent's room. When there was no answer, she knew something was wrong. That's when she took the gun and wiped the fingerprints off the ashtray." He looked at Nicole. "It must have been difficult for you, waiting to learn what had happened, keeping it to yourself."

Nicole sprang up and ran to her grandfather. "I'm sorry, Grandpère. If I had hidden the gun better—"

"I would have confessed in any event," Jean-Pierre said sadly. "Vincent Langton deserved to die, but I do not have the heart of a murderer. It is a relief to have the truth known."

Fuzz reached out to clamp handcuffs on Jean-Pierre's wrists, making it necessary for Jean-Pierre to urge his wife and granddaughter aside in order to cooperate. Everyone in the family was standing now, hovering in a semicircle around him, showing appropriate dismay over his plight. A strobe flashed as a reporter from the *Crag & Canyon*, a local weekly, captured the climactic moment on film.

Cupping Jean-Pierre's elbow, Fantasy guided him to the edge of the platform toward the exit. Brigitte broke away from the pack of Dumonts and stopped him. "Fantasy?" she began imploringly. "He's my father."

Fantasy gave her a look that might have been sympathetic. "Sorry, Babycakes. I had a job to do, and I'm doing it."

She put her hand on his arm and stepped close to him. "What's going to happen now?"

"There'll be a trial. You can cry some crocodile tears for the jury and plead for mercy. Considering his age, his standing in the community and the provocation that led him into the crime, he may get off with a probated sentence."

"Oh, Fantasy," she said miserably, and stepped into his arms for comfort.

Applause broke out as the audience recognized the closing line. Excited murmuring followed, as everyone talked about the denouement and compared the solution with their own theories. Brigitte circulated through the crowd, thanking everyone for coming and listening to their accounts of how close or how far they'd been from guessing the identity of the killer, while Charlie held court among the weekend sleuths, autographing the souvenir posters he'd designed for the event and accepting their praises for his ingenious homicide plot.

From a strictly business viewpoint, the weekend had been an unqualified success, beginning with the fully-booked crowd and ending with the substantial money raised from the auction. Brigitte had deliberately raised the opening bid on the leather jacket, knowing that one of their wealthy amateur detectives—an avid *Fantasy Fuzz* fan who was into novelty status-symbols—planned to buy it, no matter how high the bidding went.

From the standpoint of pure fun, *Death at the Dumont* had also been a roaring success. Of course, she'd probably have to endure being called Babycakes by many of their regular guests for years to come, and her family would doubtless continue to joke about Janet's red lace La Sexy Mama panties and Jean-Pierre's perfidy over many meals.

As Brigitte signed posters, she grew increasingly anxious for the last of the guests to depart. *The weekend had been an all-around success—and she could hardly wait to get Charlie alone again to let him know how personally satisfying it had been for her.*

She found him in his room, packing. "I'm supposed to extend a formal invitation to you for dinner tonight. The room's yours if you'd like to stay over."

Charlie gave the heavy zipper one final tug and met her gaze as he slung his suitcase from the rack to the floor. "I need to get home. I'm a little behind on my production schedule." He grinned. "My concentration's been off, lately." *A lot's happened in a hurry. I need space to think about it all.*

"Just how big a hurry are you in?" *Why did he make everything a challenge?*

He shrugged. "I'd like to get home by dark."

She smiled. "It's summer. The days are long."

"What'd you have in mind?" But as he asked the question, he knew. It was written on her face and in her eyes. She allowed herself to be transparent, letting him know exactly what she wanted and how he made her feel. That a woman should reveal so much to him so willingly flattered him. It also terrified him.

"Maybe if you handle all the distractions at once, you can work better when you get home."

"I guess you have a few ideas about how to distract me."

She smiled. "A few."

"The things I endure for *Fantasy Fuzz!*" Charlie said, then opened his arms to the inevitable. "Distract away, Babycakes."

She proved to be very distracting. Hours later, they were still snuggled up together in the bed. It had been a long time since either of them had uttered a word, but neither of them noticed nor particularly cared.

"I've got to hit the road soon," Charlie said at last.

Brigitte snuggled a little closer to him. Her sigh sounded suspiciously like "Stay."

"I can't." Not that it wasn't tempting. The temptation to stay right where he was, with Brigitte Dumont's delectable body cozied up against him, was very real and very strong. But so was the need to hole up alone in his artist's quarry to put everything that had happened during this crazy weekend into perspective.

Charlie wasn't accustomed to being around so many people for such an extended period of time. More significantly, he'd never had any woman get as close to him as Brigitte Dumont had. No woman had ever told him she loved him in a romantic context. No woman had ever been so frank with him. And if any woman had ever been as physically attracted to him as Brigitte apparently was, he'd never been told about it.

Yet he needed space. He needed privacy. And he needed to escape into his work and let everything that had happened between them percolate.

Brigitte sucked in a lungful of air and released it slowly. Charlie grinned. "You're the only woman I've ever met who could turn breathing into an erotic process."

Brigitte grinned back, then wriggled a bit and ran her toes along his shinbone for good measure.

"I can't stay, Brigitte," he said.

The prospect of defeat sobered her, and Brigitte pushed up on her elbow and looked down at his face. "Are you sure? You could stay for Family Night tomorrow night. We'll be talking about Death at the Dumont. We could introduce you again. It would be great PR for *Fantasy Fuzz*."

"Even if I could take the time off, I don't feel comfortable standing up like a trained bear so everyone can gawk at me."

"A trained bear, huh? Now, there's an idea. We could find you a straw hat, a tutu and an umbrella...."

"Brigitte!"

"You may be big and strong and ... eminently huggable—but no one is going to mistake you for a trained bear. If you're uncomfortable just standing up and being introduced, we can make you part of the act."

"I don't—"

His reticence seemed to feed her enthusiasm. "Oh, come on. We'll make up some crazy lyrics to one of the classics and do a soft shoe. The Fantasy Fuzz and Babycakes Shuffle. It'll be *fun*, Charlie!"

Charlie didn't think so. "I'm not a performer."

"Ha!" Brigitte exclaimed, giving him a lascivious look. "Charlie, if you were any better at performing, I'd be a withered, emaciated old woman right now."

"I was talking about dancing."

"Oh," she said innocently. "Dancing. Of course. Well, we don't do world-class ballet at the Chalet Dumont, we do vaudevillian soft shoe. Which means you don't have to be good, you just have to get up and do it. I could teach you a simple routine in half an hour."

"I have to get home, Brigitte."

"Some other time, then."

"No." He hadn't meant it to sound harsh, but he didn't mind it sounding final enough to convince her that he was serious about not doing the soft shoe.

After spending a substantial percentage of the past two days with Brigitte, Charlie should have anticipated her next strategy. Nevertheless it surprised him when she shifted so that her chest established intimate contact with his. Such a nice chest it was, too! He felt his resolve about dancing the soft shoe softening while another part of him reacted with an opposite result.

"I thought you liked dancing with me," she said.

"I do—but when we're alone, not in front of an audience. I don't like audiences much."

"The trick with audiences is to just pretend they're not there."

"*You* don't pretend they're not there," he argued, rolling toward her and pushing up on one elbow. "You love audiences. You play to them. You play off them."

"Guess it was just the way I was raised," she said blithely. "But we have some guests who aren't comfortable in front of an audience, so we tell them to pretend the audience isn't there. They say it works."

He picked up her hand and kissed it. "We're very different, Brigitte."

Either she didn't hear the warning, or she chose to ignore it, because she pressed closer to him and said, "Let's explore the differences."

"We've already explored the differences."

"Then let's explore them again and make sure they're still there."

"You're going to wear me out," Charlie complained, without conviction.

"A performer like you?" she asked.

"Talk about withered and emaciated."

Brigitte gave a throaty laugh. "You shouldn't try to lie to a woman when you're naked." She reached between them to stroke the evidence that proved his protests false.

"You're wanton," Charlie told her, then closed his eyes and sighed at the magic produced by the pressure of her fingers.

"And you're wanting," she countered.

"I have a feeling," he said, grabbing her right wrist to pull her hand away and then rolling atop her, "that wanting you could turn into a full-time avocation." Capturing her left wrist, he guided her hand close to her head, parallel with her right. He threaded his chunky fingers through her slim ones, effectively pinning her hands against the pillow. "Now, you're at my mercy."

"I've been at your mercy from the first moment you called me Babycakes."

"Are you always so honest?"

"Life's too short to dissemble."

Charlie chuckled. "Dissemble?"

Brigitte grinned. "I read it in a fortune cookie. It means—"

"I know what it means." He'd turned somber again. "But most people play games. Especially with the opposite sex."

"Do *you?*" Her eyes showed her vulnerability.

"I never learned how."

"I was never any good at those kinds of games. I've never been good at hiding things. Like feelings."

Her eyes filled with the feelings she couldn't hide, evoking his tenderness. Having a beautiful woman in love with him was still new and perplexing to him. He felt something for Brigitte that he'd never felt for any woman before. "You shouldn't look at a man like that when you're at his mercy," he said.

"I'm waiting to be ravaged," she replied, smiling.

Instead, Charlie made love to her with infinite tenderness, releasing her hands so she could reciprocate his caresses, and in the end, as they lay together struggling for breath after the tumultuous upheaval of their physical union, he realized that he was the one who'd been ravaged. He'd not been particularly happy with his solitary life-style, but he'd been content. And whether or not what he felt for her was love, and whether or not it lasted, he knew as he held her trembling body next to his own and pressed reassuring kisses on her temple that he would never be content with solitude again. With the sweet stroking of her hands, and her undemanding trust, she had given him a glimpse of what life could be without loneliness.

"What do you do when you're not organizing murder and mayhem?" he asked, suddenly curious about her life.

"I'm kind of a fairy godmother."

"Is there much call for that kind of work?"

"There is at a people-oriented hotel like the Chalet Dumont. Customers come to me wanting to put together conferences or reunions or seminars or receptions, and I try to make everything happen for them just the way they want it to happen. I also help out with PR and come up with special events that we initiate to attract business."

"Like BARF's Death at the Dumont."

She combed her fingers through his hair and smiled. "One of my first duties tomorrow will be to write you a letter officially thanking you for your participation."

"I hope you'll make it flattering."

"It'll gush with praise and gratitude. It'll extol your many virtues...."

That amused him and he smiled. "Which virtues are those?" Charlie grinned.

"Oh, let's see. Civic-mindedness. Generosity. Environmental awareness. Willingness to get involved. And after they're appropriately extolled, there's your talent to praise. That was some plot."

"That should be some letter."

"It'll be a masterpiece. I'll copy the publicist at your syndicate, of course."

"Maybe you should hand-deliver it."

"To New York?"

"My copy," Charlie said. "You know how unreliable the mails are. I'd hate to miss being extolled and praised."

"You want me—?"

"I'm asking you to visit me," he said. "You could see my studio." *See my studio, invade my space, pet my cat. Did she have any idea what a major step he'd made, inviting her into his private space?*

"I would like that," she said. "I'd like to see your studio." *I'm in love with you, but I don't know you yet. And I don't know anything about "that."* She grinned. "Are you going to show me your art prints?"

Relieved that he'd had the courage to ask and she'd agreed to visit, he caught her frivolous mood. "You're too wanton for art prints. You might get the wrong idea and try to talk me into something naughty."

"In your dreams!" she retorted, socking him playfully.

Charlie laughed. "I'll show you all the cartoon strips that didn't make it, instead."

# 13

CHARLIE PACED the floor, waiting. For the sound of a car door slamming. For a knock at the door. For the sight of a crooked smile and the music of a feminine voice.

Charlie had been glad to return home from the Chalet Dumont. But when he'd sequestered himself within the familiar rooms of his house to think and work, he'd soon discovered that the walls he'd always used to shut out the world were an ineffectual barrier to certain memories. He couldn't write "Oh, Fantasy" without hearing the words as Brigitte had said them. He couldn't draw Fantasy without his body warming at the memory of Brigitte making love to him while wearing the leather aviator jacket. He couldn't comb his hair without remembering the way she'd run her fingers through it. He couldn't shave without remembering the pressure of her fingertips on his cheek as she'd whispered, "I love you, you know."

Although he had more questions than answers where his feelings for Brigitte were concerned, not only had he caught up with his production schedule for the strip, he'd moved ahead. Sexual fulfillment enhanced creativity, he mused.

After much effort, his house was now ready to receive her. He had scrubbed basins and floors, straightened the cupboards, emptied and restocked the refrigerator, gone out and bought designer sheets in a bold geometric pattern for the bed that had suddenly seemed colorless and drab without her there to share it. He'd even rigged up a ladder to scrub the skylight above his drawing table, and polished the barbells of his weight set.

Charlie halted his pacing at the sound of an idling car engine, torn between the urge to dash outside to greet Brigitte and a paralyzing attack of nerves. Cleaning the house had been easy. Busywork. Physical. Now he was painfully aware of his inexperience as a host. The only entertaining he'd done in this house had been when he first moved in and the gang from the office at the advertising firm insisted he give them a tour. They'd come bearing food, housewarming gifts and a healthy curiosity about the private life he kept so carefully guarded.

It seemed inconceivable that he, Charlie Battle, should be standing in the middle of the room waiting for a beautiful woman to knock on his door. That he should have meat marinating and wine chilling in the refrigerator that seldom held anything more sophisticated than mustard and pickles. That he'd bought matching sheets and towels to impress her.

Through the front window, he watched her take a fold-over suit bag from the trunk of her car and start up the walk. Courtesy demanded that he offer to carry it for her and so he rushed out to meet her.

She stopped as he approached, greeting him with a slightly nervous smile, and he stood in front of her, as breathless and self-conscious as a schoolboy.

"Hi." They said it at the same time, then laughed softly.

Charlie took the bag and put his arm across her shoulders as they walked to the door. "Well," he said, once they were inside. "Welcome to *chez* Charlie."

Brigitte looked around at the living room where two huge armchairs flanked a pillowed sofa. "I like your house," she said. "It looks comfortable."

"Sit down," Charlie told her. "I'll, uh, put this bag out of the way." The ball of tension in his gut eased as he watched her settle into one of his chairs. She was no intruder in his home, but rather a comforting presence.

He returned from putting the bag in the bedroom to find her being pestered by his cat who, having found a body in the chair, had concluded, with feline logic, that the body was ripe for exploitation. The huge, rude gray tabby was perched in her lap, nosing her chin and mewing with an imperious air of urgency.

"Backagain! Get down from there!" he ordered. Backagain halted his mewing long enough to give Charlie a defiant stare, but showed no inclination to move. "Just push him away," Charlie said. "He's never learned any manners. He thinks that's his chair."

"I don't mind him," Brigitte replied, scratching the tom behind the ears. "But I never would have figured you for a cat person."

"He must have belonged to the people who sold me the house. He kept showing up, and I kept chasing him away, but every time I turned around he was back again."

"So you called him Backagain." The cat, wooed by her stroking, was now lying in her lap, head thrown back, purring loudly as she scratched its chest.

"No pride at all," Charlie remarked, giving the cat a look of disgust.

Charlie's tough-guy act didn't fool Brigitte for an instant. The cat was well fed and thoroughly spoiled, and it was obvious who did the feeding and spoiling.

"I didn't start dinner," he said. "I thought you'd want to see the studio and maybe take a walk around the block, see the neighborhood, unwind a little after your drive."

Brigitte nodded. "We've got a slight problem, though." She pointed at Backagain, who was sprawled across her lap, snoring inelegantly.

"Just dump him on the floor," Charlie advised. "He'll land on his feet and be back in the chair before you can cross the room."

But even as he said it, he cradled the sleeping cat in his hands and deposited it on the couch. Backagain stirred long enough to mew an indignant protest and ripple his spine into a position of his own choosing before going back to sleep.

"I hope you remembered to put your art prints away," Brigitte commented as they moved on to his studio. "You know how impressionable I am."

"Who needs art prints for inspiration?" Charlie guided her into his arms.

"Not I," she said, tilting her face invitingly. He kissed her gently, then held her. Brigitte burrowed her cheek against his chest. "And I was afraid you hadn't missed me."

"What makes you think I did?"

"Intuition," she replied, pushing closer against him. "And 'body Braille.'"

"You're as wanton as I remembered you."

"And you're wanting again."

"Later, Babycakes. Right now, we're about to explore the birthplace of Fantasy Fuzz and meet some of his predecessors."

"I like your skylight," Brigitte remarked, casting her gaze heavenward.

"It was the primary reason I bought the house," Charlie said, glad he'd thought to clean it. "Of course, the benefit was mostly psychological at first, since I used to do my drawing at night, after work."

The room itself was generous and square, with two drawing tables. "This table's where I do the actual work," Charlie explained. "Then, after I have the idea drafted out, I do the final product over here."

Brigitte studied the panels on the second board. Fantasy Fuzz had assembled the suspects and was pointing an accusing finger, while a kinky-curled wide-eyed Babycakes was looking on in horror. "When will this be in the paper?"

"I've got about a three-week lead time."

"Then there are people all over the world speculating on how this story will turn out?"

"Unless my readership is slipping, I would think so."

Her gaze locked with his. "You took a chance letting me see this. I could leak the identity of the killer."

"You could, but you won't."

"You wouldn't have been so sure of that a week ago."

He cradled her face in his hands and looked down at her. "I didn't know you a week ago."

"Are you sure you know me now?"

"You're here, reading the strip."

Sighing, she wrapped her arms around his waist and burrowed her forehead against his neck. "The last five days seemed like an eternity."

They kissed. He was wanting, she was wanton, the new sheets were crisp and welcoming—and dinner was several hours delayed.

At the Chalet Dumont, their time together had been stolen from the demands of the mystery weekend. Here, though, they had the luxury of using that time any way they chose.

They took a leisurely stroll to the neighborhood video outlet and rented a romantic-comedy/suspense movie for later. Then, while the meat and potatoes roasted, Charlie gave Brigitte the tour that had been aborted by their impromptu lovemaking.

Leafing through a stack of Charlie's comic strips that had never made their way into print, Brigitte observed, "All your characters are human beings."

"I like the freedom. Human beings talk, and they're mobile. And they're driven by so many emotions."

"A lot of cartoonists do animals."

"I can't see myself writing *The Bacchanalian Adventures of Backagain the Tomcat*. And I'm not comfortable putting human brains into the heads of cats or dogs or bears."

"How about elk?" Brigitte teased. "Elinor and Elven Elk, a Canadian Rocky elk couple who discover they prefer town living to the mountains and move into a condo. They're especially fond of petunia sprouts, so they grow them in a window box."

"Thank God you can't draw," Charlie said.

"But the potential for social commentary is endless," Brigitte continued, undaunted. "During rutting season, Elven could bring in a harem, which upsets the neighbors. Why, the noise alone—"

"Trust you to focus on rutting season," Charlie teased.

"Elinor, of course, would be torn between her elk instincts and the prevailing social attitudes of the town dwellers, who frown on the idea of harems."

"If there's anything worse than talking animals, it's social commentary," Charlie said. "Take my word for it, Brigitte, the world is not ready for a mountain elk in moral conflict."

"Only for a sexist genius who reduces all women to the status of mindless playthings indiscriminately referred to as 'Babycakes.'"

Charlie whistled. "Ouch! And I thought you just didn't care for mysteries."

"Surely I'm not the first to say it."

"It's been said," he admitted.

Brigitte put her hands on his forearms for emphasis. "I didn't mean anything personal. I don't want to insult you."

"Only my comic strip," he said. "But don't fret. I didn't set out to create a strip that was socially significant. I'm a cartoonist because I love the work, not because I want to change society. I'll leave society to political satirists like Garry Trudeau. I just want to make a living doing what I love to do, and I can do that by entertaining just as easily as I could by force-feeding social commentary."

"Fantasy Fuzz is a sexist," Brigitte pointed out. "That makes a comment."

"What makes a comment is the fact that he's a world-wide success. People like Fuzz because he's uncomplicated. He's fun. He's a throwback to traditional values. Men envy him and women fantasize about him. They can be comfortable with him because he doesn't actually exist."

"Humph!" Brigitte said.

"Just don't confuse me with my cartoon character," Charlie warned. "He's not a self-portrait."

Lifting her fingertips to caress his cheek, she smiled sweetly and said, "If I thought he was, I'd knee you in the groin the next time you called me Babycakes."

"Come on," he said, wrapping his fingers firmly around her upper arm. "With that attitude you're going to love the next stop on this tour."

"The torture chamber?" she quipped.

Charlie flung open the door to the weight room. "In a manner of speaking. This is where I work off all my frustration."

Brigitte looked at all the paraphernalia—from the racked barbells to the weight bench. "You must have a lot of frustration to work off if you need all this equipment."

"Most of it was my father's," he explained. "He was really into weights, even before it was fashionable."

"I guess cops have to stay in shape."

"My mom wanted to throw them out when we left Chicago, but I wouldn't hear of it." He wrapped his fingers around the barbell on the rack. "Some of my earliest memories are of watching my father press weights. I thought he was a giant."

He shrugged his shoulders, sloughing away the memories. "So my mother and I made a deal. I could keep the weight stuff, but only if I used it. So I did."

"And with spectacular results," Brigitte remarked, playfully sizing his biceps with her fingers.

"Those results took a while," Charlie said. "I was a pretty puny kid." *Puny. Awkward. Shy. An insignificant blur lost in the shadow of a larger-than-life father who lived a hero's life and died a hero's death.*

Charlie consoled himself with the belief that had his father lived, he would have guided him into manhood, easing his transition from child to adult, counseling him. But his father hadn't lived. He'd died when Charlie most needed a strong man to show him the way. So he'd been left feeling abandoned and inadequate. He hadn't measured up to the man, and now he stood no chance of measuring up to the memory. So he'd fled his inadequacies and insecurities by avoiding people and channeling his energy into his art and working off his frustration in the weight room.

Brigitte examined the barbell suspended in the hooks. "What's your max?"

"Two thirty."

"I'm impressed."

"Don't be. It's fair to middling."

*And how much could your father press?* she wondered. She'd better not ask. Instead, she rose on tiptoe to kiss Charlie's cheek. "You're a fascinating man, Charlie Battle."

Charlie grinned. "What'd I do to deserve that?"

"You put together whatever it is that's producing that aroma. I'm starving."

"Let's go see if it's ready to dish up," Charlie said.

After dinner they cuddled up on the sofa and watched the movie, finishing off the bottle of wine they'd opened with their meal. Stretched out next to Charlie, Brigitte was so disinclined to move as the final credits rolled over the television screen that she protested the movement of his arm as he pointed the remote control at the set to rewind the film.

"Let's just stay here," she said. "Forever."

"We'd both have cricks in our necks before morning."

"We'll worry about that in the morning."

He kissed the top of her head and traced her lips with his fingertip. "I'm sure you'll think of something better to do in the morning—provided you don't have the distraction of a crick in the neck."

"Are you pandering to my baser instincts?"

"It seems to be the only way I'm going to get off this sofa and into that comfortable bed."

"You could carry me."

"Just remember you asked for it," he said, rolling out from under her so quickly that she landed on the sofa with a jolt. Then, before she could react, she was draped over his shoulder.

"This wasn't exactly what I had in mind," she complained as her nose bounced against his shoulder blades.

"Gripe, gripe, gripe!" he said. "And would you please quit wiggling."

"Neanderthal!"

His hand landed on her vulnerable behind with a resounding *thwack*. "Happy to oblige."

"You're about as romantic as an aardvark!" she said as he tossed her onto the bed.

Charlie pulled his shirt over his head and tossed it savagely aside. Then, fixing his gaze on Brigitte, he leaped onto the bed and lunged for her. Grabbing her wrists, he pinned her hands above her head. "It's not good strategy to insult a man who can bench twice your body weight."

His crotch pressed into hers intimately, and she felt the hardness of his body against her. He was swelling in response to the contact. Her own body warmed and grew taut with desire. "I'm quivering," she said.

"Not in fear?" he teased.

She lifted her hips, straining against him, begrudging the clothes that separated them. "No."

"Wanton wench!" he replied, lowering his head for a claiming kiss. He lifted his mouth from hers to look into her eyes. "Damn it! You've got me quivering too!" Greedy for the feel of her hands on his flesh, he released them and resumed kissing her.

BRIGITTE WAS AWAKENED the next morning by a gentle but persistent nudging. She opened one eye to behold a hairy gray beast crouched on her chest and a whiskered muzzle in her face.

"Backagain," she groaned, pushing him off so she could raise herself up on one elbow. "Are you supposed to be in here?"

Backagain mewed indignantly. "Where's Charlie?" Brigitte asked. The last thing she remembered was cuddling up in his arms, utterly replete from their lovemaking. She must have been semicomatose not to have stirred when he left the bed.

A smile curled her lips. No small wonder, after the night they'd spent together. She glanced at the clock on the headboard. Almost ten. He might have been up for hours. Sighing, she made her way to the bathroom. It would have been nice to wake up with his warm body beside her, but privacy had a certain appeal. Who knows, maybe he was in the living room, just waiting to make breakfast.

One shower later, she pulled on the satin lounge shirt she'd not had the opportunity to wear since her arrival and went in search of her host. A quick check of the kitchen eliminated the prospect of breakfast, unless he'd decided to run out for fresh bagels. Then a faint clanking sound caught her attention, and she set off in the direction of its origin. Charlie was in the weight room, pressing at the bench.

He lowered the barbell onto the brace. "I thought I heard you moving around."

For the first time in his life he'd awakened with the pleasant awareness of a woman's naked body next to his, but she'd been sleeping so soundly he hadn't wanted to disturb her. Though he knew he should be exhausted from the night they'd shared, he'd been filled with restless energy. He'd tried briefly to go back to sleep and hadn't been able to, so he'd gently extricated himself from the woman who seemed loath for him to move away, even as she slept. After skimming the Sunday paper, he'd still been restless, so he'd wandered to the weight room to do his every-other-day routine.

"Backagain decided it was time for me to get up."

"Damned cat must be jealous."

"Must be," Brigitte replied.

"Do you mind if I finish my workout? I have a routine."

"Sure. Go ahead."

Charlie waited for her to leave. She didn't. Instead she asked, "Mind if I watch?"

Actually, Charlie did mind. Since he had his own equipment, he'd never belonged to a spa where there were people around, and he wasn't entirely comfortable with an audience, especially an audience of one woman who had just climbed out of his bed. It had been a stretch for him to show her this room; he hadn't bargained on her being here when he worked out. Still, it seemed inhospitable to kick her out, so he shrugged and said, "Go ahead. Watch."

Brigitte didn't merely watch. She walked around him in slow circles, studying him the way she might a piece of sculpture in a museum. She appeared to be fascinated by the rippling of his muscles as he strained with the weights. Charlie felt his concentration eroding and gritted his teeth, hoping that she'd lose interest and leave.

"Why don't you make yourself useful," he suggested. "Add twenty on each end."

"Sure." She approached the task with her usual vigor, giggling when one pin stubbornly refused to snap, but persevering until it was in place. "You're on," she said.

Charlie looked up at the stem of the barbell, envisioning himself lifting it. He took several deep breaths and raised his hands, positioning them carefully, focusing his energy on the act of lifting.

Brigitte observed all this with fascination, aroused by the power of his body and the force of his concentration.

With the awareness of a lover, she followed the line of his thighs to the hem of his shorts, and her mind envisioned what his clothing concealed. Unable to resist, she reached out to touch that straining thigh muscle.

The violence of his reaction astounded her. The barbell landed in the braces with a metallic crash, and Charlie shouted a curse she hadn't heard since Stephen had been frustrated over his confinement to a wheelchair following his accident. He was breathing heavily, from exertion and nervous reaction.

"You could kill a man doing that!"

"I'm sorry," she said meekly.

"I could have dropped this thing on my neck or my chest—even my head."

"I just wanted to feel—"

"Half of weight lifting is concentration."

Embarrassed, Brigitte stared at the far wall to avoid looking at Charlie. "I said I was sorry. I won't touch you again."

"Just...don't surprise me." He could tell from the droop of her shoulders that she was hurt. "I didn't mean to snap," he told her, and exhaled a sigh of frustration. "You scared the hell out of me!"

"It won't happen again!"

"Brigitte—"

"It's okay. Really. I'm just a little embarrassed. Just...go back to concentrating."

Charlie frowned and went back to his pressing, positioning his hands and trying to imagine the barbells off the rack. He took several deep breaths.

Satisfied that he was absorbed in his weight work, she watched him lift the barbell from the rack. *Concentration, huh? We'll just see how good your concentration is, Mr. Battle.*

Charlie noted with relief that she walked out of the room, and was so involved in his pressing that he didn't hear her return. He was alerted to her presence only as the blue of her satin shirt caught his eye as she moved into his field of peripheral vision. He'd done two repetitions by the time she'd walked to the end of the bench and stopped there.

He lost his timing and parked the barbell. "Just ignore me," she said. "Go on with whatever . . ."

Charlie cast her a dubious look, but started his breathing to reestablish his timing. His hands were pressing against the sleeve of the barbell, just beginning to feel the pressure of the lift, when she grasped the tails of the shirt and pulled it up over her head, and off. He let the barbell fall back onto the racks. He'd always prided himself on his concentration, but he'd never tried to concentrate on a mindless, brute effort with a naked woman standing in front of him.

"You're lucky I'm not throwing this thing at you," he said.

"*That's* not why I'm lucky," she replied, climbing astride him on the bench. Her breasts compressed against his ribs as she leaned forward to drop a row of kisses along his collarbone. Her thighs caressed him through his shorts, pressing into his buttocks.

Overwhelmed by sensation, Charlie started to embrace her, but she grabbed his wrists and guided his hands back to the barbell and gave him a wicked smile. "Now you're at *my* mercy."

Charlie couldn't have resisted her if both their lives had depended on it. She was already too close to him. His body was responding to her touch with terrifying intensity. He shifted his hips to adjust the clothing binding him and she gasped, wriggling above him in response. She went wild kissing him, pressing her lips and tongue to his skin, sucking and nibbling. Combing her fingers into his hair, she used her breasts to tease and beguile while she fused her mouth with his. Arching her back, she presented her breasts to him, begging him with teasing movements to take them into his mouth while she strained forward to nibble on his ear.

The sounds she made—little gasps and groans of wanting—had an erotic effect. By the time she tugged at the elastic band of his shorts with anxious fingers and followed them with hot, moist lips, he was lost to anything except Brigitte and the feelings she aroused in him. Her fingers stroked and squeezed, as she put a condom on him. Then she lowered herself over him, guiding him inside her, and moaned with pleasure as she received him.

She moved frantically on top of him, drawing him deep into the rhythm leading to sensual fulfillment. Charlie gripped the sleeve of the barbell for support as her frenzied lovemaking drove him over the peak and spasms of release racked his body. He heard Brigitte cry out as her fingers grasped his shoulders in a desperate grip, and she strained against him while she took the same ecstatic plunge.

Struggling for breath, she collapsed against him, her cheek on his chest. Then, with her palms braced on his shoulders, she pushed up to look down at him. Her face told him she was as overwhelmed as he; as surprised. He'd never seen anything as beautiful as that face, or anyone as totally vulnerable as she.

Only extraordinary strength enabled him to pull up into a sitting position so he could cradle her in his arms. Shivering, she wrapped her arms around him and clung to him. She tilted her head back to look at him beseechingly, and he cradled her cheeks in his palms and gently kissed her face.

They held each other for a long time. Brigitte rested her cheek in that inviting crook where Charlie's neck met his shoulder and listened while Charlie's heart slowed to its normal rate.

"I knew you didn't want me here, but you were so . . . I wanted—"

He whispered the expletive he'd said earlier, making it sound strangely like an endearment, and pulled her closer. "It's all right. Better than that. It was incredible."

"It was a fantasy," she said, raising her head to kiss him briefly on the lips. "Thank you for sharing it."

"Brigitte?"

She looked at him inquiringly.

"Don't ever come into this room again," he said.

She understood what he meant. She had trespassed into a private place where he'd felt safe and comfortable and totally in control.

She flashed him a brilliant smile. "That would be anticlimactic, wouldn't it?"

# 14

"A CONGA LINE at Family Night?" Claire asked.

"Sure," Brigitte replied. "Why not? We've never done one. You could handle that on the kazoos, couldn't you, Janet. Dah-dah-dah-dah-dah-dah!"

"I guess so."

"It's settled, then. Now all we have to do is get Mother to work out some chords, and find someone who knows the basic steps."

"I hope Charlie gets back from Chicago soon," Claire said. "You're losing your grip on reality."

"I've heard sexual deprivation impairs judgment," Janet added. "Of course, with your brother around, I wouldn't know anything about that."

"You guys are a barrel of laughs," Brigitte remarked. "The conga will be a hit. Wait and see."

After posting a notice on the bulletin board in the resident staff's dormitory, Brigitte located a housekeeping assistant who not only knew the conga but was thrilled to demonstrate it and lead the line, which, on Family Night, snaked through the dining room, weaving among the tables, for a full twenty minutes.

When it broke up Brigitte, near exhaustion, returned to the family table, keenly anticipating the pleasure of giving Claire a healthy sibling-to-sibling I-told-you-so. Reaching for her water glass, she discovered a Chalet Dumont envelope propped against it. "What's this?"

"According to the bellboy, it's for your eyes only," Stephen said. "He was prepared to chase you down and give it to you, but I assured him I'd see that you got it as soon as you recovered from your bout of Latin American dance fever."

The handwriting on the front of the envelope was unmistakable. "It's from Charlie."

"Don't open it in here. Anything that confidential could burst into flames when it hits the air."

"Good thinking, brother of mine!" Brigitte said, clutching the letter to her bosom as she sprang from her chair. "Get Claire to cover for me if I don't come back?"

"Playing hard to get, eh?"

She gave him a jaunty lift of an eyebrow. "That depends on what the note says!"

It had been almost a month since her visit to Charlie's house. When she left him then, he'd been planning to visit her at the chalet two weekends hence. Then there had been a tense call of apology. The City of Chicago had decided to declare Fantasy Fuzz an honorary citizen and give his creator the key to the city at a special mayor's breakfast.

They'd agreed to postpone their date a week. But then there'd been a second phone call, even more apologetic. Charlie had sounded restless and frustrated as he explained that the publicist from the syndicate was making a circus of the trip, setting up press conferences, talk shows and guest appearances. Charlie wasn't sure when he'd get back to Banff, but he assured Brigitte he was miserable. He hated working out in the hotel fitness room with unfamiliar equipment and strange people all around. That evoked a significant "Hmm" from Brigitte, and he'd exhibited enough largesse to concede that he'd even allow her back into his weight room if he could just get home. As an afterthought, he added that he missed her. Brigitte was touched enough to confess that she'd missed him a bit, too.

And now he was at the chalet. She tore open the envelope to find a cartoon depiction of a pair of elk making goo-goo eyes at each other and sparking hearts and exclamations points. Eloquent as ever, Charlie had written only his room number and the admonition, "Use your pass-key."

She scarcely needed the elevator to get to the fourth floor. After knocking at the door, she used her passkey. The room was totally dark, with lights out and shades tightly drawn. Reaching for the wall switch, she found it covered with tape. She gasped as someone lunged out of the darkness and grabbed her around the waist and pushed the door shut, then exhaled a sigh of relief as she recognized the strong body she was pinned against and the scent of Charlie's after-shave. "You scared the—"

"Shh." He covered her mouth with his. And in total darkness, while never breaking the kiss, he undressed her, scooped her naked body into his arms with the finesse of Errol Flynn in his prime and carried her to the bed.

Slipping between the covers with her, he pulled her into his arms and made love to her slowly and thoroughly. An hour later, as they lay utterly replete and on the verge of sleep, he whispered, "I love you, Babycakes."

BRIGITTE WOKE UP the next morning thinking that perhaps she'd imagined the whole episode until she felt Charlie next to her—warm, very real, and sleeping soundly. Gingerly she left the bed and donned enough of her clothing not to be embarrassed if she met anyone in the hall. With a grin, she pulled the masking tape off the light switch and hung the Do Not Disturb sign on the door on her way out, equally concerned over Charlie's sleep and a certain telltale piece of lingerie she hadn't been able to locate in the darkness and would prefer a maid didn't find by light of day.

She dressed for work and fairly floated into the lobby, ready for anything life or the clients of the Chalet Dumont threw her way. Claire was at the front desk, supervising a new employee. "Good morning," Brigitte said.

Claire excused herself and followed Brigitte into her office. "That good-morning was obscenely cheerful."

Brigitte answered with a wry smile.

"How's Charlie?"

"Still a man of few words." *The right words.*

"Did he happen to mention how he passed his time in Chicago?"

"We didn't do much talking," Brigitte said. "Why do you ask?"

"It's probably quite innocent."

"What is?"

"Our weekly newsmagazines came in this morning. Charlie made the cover."

"That's great. Which one?"

*"Faces."*

Brigitte whistled. "His publicist will be in ecstasy. I'll have to take him a copy." *With a breakfast tray, perhaps. Croissants and marmalade and fresh strawberries—*

"Brigitte—"

She looked at her sister, and Claire said, "He wasn't alone."

"What do you mean?" Brigitte demanded, trying, unsuccessfully to keep her anxiety from showing.

"He was wearing the Fuzz Jacket, and there was an actress posing as Babycakes."

"Blond?" Brigitte asked.

Claire nodded gravely. "A soap-opera siren."

"A soap-opera siren," Brigitte repeated with deadly calm.

"It's probably just a publicity shot. You know how publicists are."

*Just a publicity shot.* The picture of her and Charlie in *Contemporary Canada* had been just a publicity shot! She rose. "I think I'd better have a look."

If there was any consolation, it was that they weren't kissing. But that was small consolation, considering that the soap-opera siren was wearing a trench coat with a flipped-up collar and a neckline that plunged almost to her navel, revealing enough cleavage for a small army to get lost in; and she had one hand on Charlie's chest and the other hand in his hair.

Brigitte rolled up the magazine and stalked across the lobby from the newsstand to the housekeeping storage area where she picked up an ice bucket before heading for the elevator. She filled the bucket at the ice machine on Charlie's floor, then had to juggle it and the magazine while she used her master key to get into his room. Once inside, she opened the drapes.

Charlie was sleeping soundly, looking boyish with his hair tousled. Hardening her heart against that boyish charm, Brigitte marched to the bed, flung back the bedding and emptied the ice bucket dead center between his chest and his knees.

Gasping and sputtering, Charlie sprang up, then began cursing. Spying Brigitte he demanded, "What the hell—?"

"This!" Brigitte held the magazine out at arm's length, shoving it in his face.

Sleep-dazed, Charlie scrambled out of bed, away from the ice. He yanked the top sheet from the bed and wrapped it around him, then took the magazine from Brigitte. "They ran it this week."

"Is that all you're going to say? *They ran it this week?*"

Charlie yawned. "Guess the politician didn't die."

"Ooooo-ooo," Brigitte groaned in exasperation. "I should have known better than to fall in love with someone named Charlie."

"What's my name got to do with anything?"

"You're on the cover of an American magazine with an...*actress* after we, you and I... And the only thing you have to say is that some politician didn't die."

"The former majority whip of the U. S. Senate had a stroke and was lingering. They had a memorial portrait all set to run with an obituary feature if he died, and they said they'd have to bump our cover if he went by press time."

"Charlie! I don't give a damn when they ran the blasted cover. I want to know what you were doing playing Babycakes with a soap-opera siren in Chicago after making love to me on your weight bench."

"You're jealous?" he asked, as though the possibility had never occurred to him. "You don't think that I... that Lauren and I—?"

"I don't have to think! I can see. The entire North American continent can see it in full color on the cover of *Faces* magazine. I just hope you enjoyed it, because—" The unspoken threat was quite clear.

"You think I enjoyed working with Lauren?"

"I rather thought you enjoyed 'working' with me."

"That's because you're ... you."

Brigitte's outrage lessened as she observed him. He was so sincere. Surely no one would pretend to be so naive and expect anyone to buy it.

"You smell good," Charlie said, instinctively pressing his advantage. "Lauren smelled like a funeral parlor. You know—like old flowers."

Brigitte would have been willing to bet the chalet that that funeral-parlor scent came in a fancy bottle and cost Lauren no less than two hundred dollars an ounce.

"And you kissed me like you enjoyed kissing me, and you tasted...like a woman ought to taste, I guess. Lauren wore so much makeup it was like trying to kiss an oil painter's palette. And she had to have everything choreographed so that her good side was to the audience and there were no shadows on her face."

"It must have been a living hell for you."

Charlie missed the irony entirely. "If it had been anyone but the 100 Club of Cook County, I'd have turned them down flat."

"The 100 Club?"

"They help families of police officers who are wounded or killed. They gave my mother the money to move and helped with her tuition so she could finish college. They even helped with my tuition when I started college."

"I guess it would have been tough to turn them down," Brigitte grudgingly agreed.

"Lauren's father is a bigwig in the 100 Club. He used to be an officer with Chicago P.D. before he left to start a private security firm. Didn't they put all that in the article?"

"I only read the first paragraph," Brigitte confessed. "Damn it, Charlie, the picture was enough. You could have warned me it was coming."

"I was going to tell you all about it."

"Well, why didn't you?"

Charlie risked putting his hands on her shoulders. "I didn't feel like talking last night."

"Humph!"

"I was going nuts, surrounded by people all the time. All I wanted last night—" since he hadn't been rebuffed for touching her, he guided her into an embrace "—was you. You said the weight bench was a fantasy for you. Last night was a fantasy for me. No talking, no words, just—"

He let action finish his statement, hugging her, then he sighed with relief when she relaxed against him.

"It's just a good thing that the few words you did say last night were the right ones," she said.

"I meant them."

"Even better." She tilted her head back, inviting his kiss.

Charlie accepted the invitation, but kept the kiss sweet and unhurried. "I'm sorry I didn't tell you about the cover. Can I make it up to you?"

Brigitte pretended to ponder the question. "I suppose you could grovel at my feet and beg my forgiveness."

The look he gave her took her breath away. "I'd rather kiss your knees until your legs buckle."

"That would do it," Brigitte replied, her throat suddenly dry.

"Uh-hmm," Charlie said. "But first . . ."

When he lifted his mouth from hers again, Brigitte commented, "You're getting pretty good with zippers. Are you sure you didn't do some practicing in Chicago?"

Charlie guided her dress down over her hips. Brigitte picked it up and tossed it over a chair. "I'm going to need this . . . Charlie!"

Charlie kissed his way down her midriff to the edge of her panties. Pushing them down, he followed their path down her thighs with his palms until he reached her knees. "I've never made a woman's legs buckle before."

"You must have a natural talent for it," Brigitte said shakily as he touched his lips to her kneecap. It was exquisite torture having his mouth on her knee while his fingers returned to caress her thigh. When he moved to the other leg and kissed his way up her thigh, she sighed languidly. "They're buckling, Charlie."

Straightening, he looked down at her and grinned devilishly before grabbing her shoulders and pulling her to him for a reckless kiss. By the time he scooped her up into his arms, she was thinking of nothing but the feel of his body against hers and the driving need he'd built in her.

It took a few seconds to register the chill of the melting ice into which he tossed her and realize he'd deliberately set her up for retribution. She shrieked with laughter.

Charlie laughed heartily as she scrambled away from the cold, wet mass. Incensed, she grabbed the edge of the sheet wrapped around him and tugged as hard as she could. Caught off guard, Charlie stumbled against the edge of the bed and fell forward onto it. Brigitte picked up a handful of ice cubes and rubbed them over his bare back. Gasping, Charlie looped his arm around her waist and reciprocated. Brigitte squealed in protest and squirmed away from him. She almost made it to the foot of the bed, but Charlie grabbed her ankle to tether her. Brigitte gathered the bedspread into a ball and flung it at him to distract him and kicked to free her ankle. Charlie lunged at her and they slid, bedspread and all, to the floor.

They landed nose to nose. "This is another fine mess you've gotten us into," Brigitte said.

"You started it."

"I was provoked."

"You overreacted."

"You got revenge."

Charlie chuckled. "Yes."

"Bully!"

"Spitfire!"

Brigitte moved her leg in a way that put her lower body in intimate alignment with his. Her voice took on a lustful tone. "Brute!"

"Brat." He pressed his chest against her bare breasts.

"You were supposed to be making my legs buckle."

"Wanton as ever, aren't you?"

"I've heard there are sexy things you can do with ice."

"Like what?"

"I don't have the foggiest idea."

"Then I guess we're just going to have to do it the old-fashioned way."

"Do what?" she asked, feigning innocence.

"What we do so well," he said, dipping his head to kiss her.

BRIGITTE ALMOST FORGOT her ten-thirty appointment, but luckily Claire had paged her. Since the meeting ran long, it was well after noon before she met Charlie for lunch in the Chalet Dumont dining room.

"You should have come in for Family Night last night," Brigitte told him. "We had a conga line."

"I heard the commotion from the-lobby," Charlie said. "I wasn't in the mood."

"Umm," Brigitte replied.

"I just wanted some peace and quiet."

Brigitte smiled sweetly. "We both know what you were in the mood for."

"I wasn't the only one."

"I wasn't complaining."

They ate in silence for a few minutes. "Tell me about Chicago," said Brigitte. "Was the mystery weekend a sell-out there?"

"Instantly. Joe Blanning—he's the publicist from the syndicate—wasn't sure they could put it together on such short notice, but when he mentioned the idea to the president of the 100 Club, they went for it and got the word out, and it was booked up within hours. Most of the members are businessmen, and they're all interested in police work. When Lauren's father heard about it, he naturally thought it would be good PR for her to play Babycakes."

"Naturally."

"It wasn't my idea," Charlie said defensively.

"No. It was BARF's idea to have a mystery weekend and have you play Fantasy Fuzz. Your publicist ripped it off, big time."

"It wasn't the same scenario," Charlie told her. "The victim in this one was a member of the 100 Club and the officers of the club were suspect. They weren't as used to being in front of an audience as your family was."

"Then you were lucky to have a pro playing Babycakes, weren't you?"

"How many times do I have to say it, Brigitte? I didn't . . . enjoy working with her the way we . . . you and I—"

"If I'd thought you had, you wouldn't have been kissing my knees." She put down her fork and sighed. "Look, Charlie, I consider myself to be a relatively sophisticated woman, but I have a tough enough time dealing with this Babycakes thing even when it's just you and me."

"Babycakes has nothing to do with you and me."

She gave him an exasperated look. "It was a shock seeing you with another woman on that cover, Charlie. I know we don't have any agreements or anything, and I don't have any right to ask you not to play Fantasy Fuzz, but I'm not sure I'll ever get used to the idea of your running around playing with gorgeous blondes."

"God, this is ironic," Charlie said. "You couldn't find a man with a more negligible social life than mine. It's not as though I've spent my adult life surrounded by women."

"Only last week, in Chicago."

"It's not likely to happen again. I did BARF because it was local, and I believe in it. I did the 100 Club because they helped my mother and me after my father was killed. But I don't plan on making a career of playing Fantasy Fuzz. I'm perfectly happy just drawing him."

"So, what else did you do?" Brigitte asked, content to change the subject.

"*Oprah Winfrey.* You should have been there. She had a homicide detective, an editor, Lauren and a feminist on with me, all discussing Fantasy Fuzz. You'd have been right at home spouting off about how sexist Fuzz is."

"Petite brunettes spend their lives avoiding being photographed with statuesque blondes."

"You're twice—ten times—as pretty as she is," Charlie told her.

Tears stung Brigitte's eyes as she looked across the table at him. "You don't say a lot, Charlie, but what you say is usually on target."

"You aren't going to cry, are you?"

"If I do, it's only because I love you so much." *You big lummox!*

# 15

WHEN BRIGITTE ARRIVED on Charlie's doorstep for a weekend visit, shivering from the chill of early-fall dusk, Charlie made a ceremony of laying the first fire of the season. Then he turned off the lights and they cuddled up on the sofa, contentedly watching the flames dance over the logs.

"Joe Blanning called yesterday," Charlie said.

Brigitte detected a note of tension in his voice. "The publicist from the syndicate?"

Charlie paused as he drew in a fortifying breath. "He wants to set up a mystery weekend in New York City to benefit a major cancer-research facility."

"Who's playing Babycakes?" Brigitte asked with an uneasy feeling.

Charlie hesitated again. "I wanted to talk to you about that."

"I figured as much from the way you led into it. Who'd they get?"

"No one, yet."

"Don't tell me Meryl Streep was busy. Have they heard from Michelle Pfeiffer?"

"I told him I'd do it under one condition."

"The cover of *Newsweek*?" she suggested, letting her head fall back against his chest.

"You're not making this easy."

His forearm was resting on her ribs. She drew circles on it with her forefinger. "I'm your jealous lover. I'm supposed to make your life difficult. But I'll nibble—what's the condition?"

"That Brigitte Dumont plays Babycakes."

She sat up and twisted around to give him an incredulous look. "That's some condition."

"Celebrities have clout," Charlie stated almost bitterly.

"What did they say?"

Charlie grinned. "He seemed to think there was a certain human-interest angle in your participation."

*You know what he means?* A public revelation of their relationship. Exploitation. Invasion of their privacy—the privacy Charlie protected so zealously.

Charlie nodded gravely.

Brigitte looked him squarely in the eye. "Are you ready for that?"

"I'd rather go public with our relationship than jeopardize it by agreeing to something that makes you uncomfortable. Either we do it together, or I don't do it at all."

She rolled over so that she could see him without straining. "So, what are we going to tell them?"

"Tell who?"

"The reporters." She spoke into an imaginary microphone in a deep voice. "Tell me, Mr. Battle, you and Ms. Dumont seem to be an item. What is the nature of your relationship?"

She shoved the imaginary microphone under his nose. Charlie grinned. "Strictly nonplatonic."

"Are your intentions toward her honorable?"

He looked down at his lap. "Not when she has her thigh draped across mine."

"Given your propensity for...*carnality* where Ms. Dumont is concerned, are you planning to do the honorable thing by her?"

"No comment."

Brigitte crawled onto his lap and sat up, resting her bottom on the tops of his thighs. "You said you were ready to go public with our relationship."

"I thought that would please you."

"It does," she said quickly, tenderly touching his cheek with her fingertips. "I'm flattered and thrilled, but . . . Charlie, they'd ask a lot of probing questions. We've never talked about the future. It's going to be obvious that we're more than casually involved. What would you say if they asked where our relationship is headed?"

"No comment."

"No comment?" She appeared stricken, as though he'd dealt her a physical blow.

"We wouldn't have to answer any personal questions," he said nervously.

All teasing was gone from her voice when she asked, "What would you say if I asked that question?"

Fearful of saying the wrong thing, Charlie hesitated. "You know how I feel about you."

"Where *are* we headed, Charlie?"

"I've never felt this way about a woman."

"I didn't ask you how you felt, Charlie. I asked where we're headed."

*He'd told her he loved her—what else could she want?* "Are you talking about getting married or something?"

"You've already had the 'or something,'" Brigitte pointed out. "You've had a lot of 'or something.'" If he'd made a joke of it, made up some preposterous destination for an answer, she could have dealt with it. His obliviousness cut to the quick. Was the idea of marriage such a shock to him? Hadn't it ever crossed his mind?

"You make it sound like I've been raiding a cookie jar. It wasn't all me, you know. In fact—"

Brigitte sighed forlornly. "I haven't been direct enough, I guess."

"If you'd been any more direct, I might not have survived that interlude on the weight bench."

She frowned. "I'm talking about our relationship, and you're talking about great sex."

"It's all mixed together, isn't it?"

"One is part of the other—at least for me." Her shoulders sagged. "I can see how you— The mixed messages—

"What else would you expect from someone whose father was a playboy and whose mother was a twenty-year-old virgin? How were you supposed to know which half of me you were interacting with?

"The sex," she continued, commanding his full attention. "That was my father's legacy—passion is part of my nature. But the love... When I told you I loved you, you thought it was part of the physical thing, and who could blame you?"

"I knew it was more. I knew you meant it."

"But you didn't know what I meant by it. I just don't love being with you, Charlie— I love you. The happily-ever-after, 'forever' kind."

He held out his hands as if to shield himself. "Whoa! Brigitte—?"

"See! Oh, God, Charlie, I knew it would take you a while to get around to it, but then you told me you loved me, and I thought you sensed... But then, how could you? With Jean-Pierre Dumont's daughter coming at you like a sex-starved concubine, it must have been easy not to realize that Marguerite Dumont's daughter was fantasizing about white lace."

"Among other things," Charlie said dryly.

"Among other things—like converting a top-floor corner room of the chalet into a studio for you. Things like how sweet it would be to sleep with you every night and wake up with you next to me, and know I had a right to expect you there." Her voice faltered, but she went on weakly. "Things like what our children would look like."

Charlie raised his hand to wipe away her tears with his thumbs. "Brigitte. I never realized—"

"That hurts most of all," she murmured, and dropped her head to his chest, sobbing softly against his shirt.

Charlie did his best to soothe her, stroking her back and kissing the top of her head, uttering vague phrases of reassurance. What was he supposed to say to her? A woman like Brigitte—giving, loving, beautiful—deserved everything she was hungering after. Love. Fidelity. *Marriage and family.*

Sharing his life—creating new life—how could the thought of it be so scary with a woman like Brigitte, who gave her love so unreservedly? But scary it was. Terrifying. It brought to mind memories of another time when he'd been terrified—of the day he'd learned that his father had been killed. He'd experienced the same sense of upheaval that day, the same feeling that everything was out of control, the same apprehension of the unknown.

The sobs had subsided. Brigitte turned her head so she faced air instead of his chest.

Charlie said her name. She closed her eyes and sighed, listening to the sound of his heart under her ear, and grew very still, waiting.

Charlie would have cut off a limb to be able to tell her what she wanted to hear. But she was honest, and she deserved the truth. "I care more about you than I've ever cared about any woman," he told her.

"My clock's ticking, Charlie. If you listened real hard you could hear it. I can't go on being the Sweetheart of the Chalet Dumont forever."

He combed his fingers into her hair and cradled her scalp. "You're not that old."

Her eyes reflected profound seriousness. "I want the things a woman wants out of life. I want stability, Charlie."

"I—"

"Don't say anything, please. It was obvious from the look on your face that you've never thought about anything beyond the moment. This isn't a mercy plea for commitment."

Charlie winced. "There are times when it would be easier if you weren't so open and direct."

"It's time to think about it, Charlie. About us. We can't just go on commuting back and forth like this until I gradually become the Chalet Dumont spinster. I won't let that happen. I want a man full-time." She met his gaze directly. "I want babies."

"Why don't you find a club and bludgeon me over the head? It would be more subtle."

"Think about it, Charlie." She let that sink in before concluding, softly, "Sooner or later, you're either going to have to make an honest woman of me or let me find a man who will."

THE TROUBLING confrontation cast a pall over the rest of Brigitte's visit. They went to a movie, but it failed to amuse. They made love, but their lovemaking was tinged with bittersweetness.

Brigitte was almost relieved when it was time to leave and Charlie walked her to her car on Sunday afternoon. Once her bag was in the trunk, they stood next to the car, awkwardly avoiding each other's eyes.

After a long silence, Brigitte asked, "How important is this thing in New York?"

"Joe says it would be great PR."

"What about the syndicate? Are you under pressure from them to do it?"

"They don't own me, but I like to accommodate them when I can. Without them, *Fantasy Fuzz* would be just one more discarded idea in that stack in my studio. I don't have a lot of faith in this PR stuff, but the weekend would raise a lot of money for the cancer hospital, and I don't mind lending my name to a worthy cause."

"When do you have to call them?"

"As soon as possible. By the end of the week at the latest."

Brigitte grew quiet, which Charlie read as an ominous sign. Finally she shifted restlessly. "It's not fair to put this decision on my shoulders. It could affect your relationship with your syndicate and cost you an important PR opportunity."

"What do you want from me, Brigitte?" Charlie asked. "I'm not going to do it with another woman playing Babycakes." He grinned. "You might decide to come after me with a pot of hot coffee instead of ice."

She shook her head in exasperation. Needing to touch her, he capped her shoulders with his palms. "Why don't you think it over and give me a call in the middle of the week."

"Why don't you drive in for Family Night tomorrow night so we can talk about it some more."

"Brigitte—" he began.

"I see," she cut in sharply.

Charlie's guts constricted. *What now? Lord, weren't things bad enough?* "What do you see?"

"You're willing to 'go public' with our relationship on your turf, but you're not ready to walk on mine."

She'd driven him to his wit's end. "What's that supposed to mean?"

"Mystery weekends are what *you* do!" Brigitte fumed. "You're fine when you're running around pretending to be Fantasy Fuzz, and your darling detective is the center of attention. Well, Family Night is what *I* do. It's part of my life, the way *Fantasy Fuzz* is part of yours."

Stiffening her spine, she planted her hands on her hips. "You were fine at Family Night when we were singing about Fantasy Fuzz and I was playing Babycakes. But even then, when the center of attention shifted, you took off. I asked you to stay over for Family Night that weekend, and you took off again."

"You wanted me to get up and *dance!*"

They exchanged scowls. Charlie felt the heat of Brigitte's outrage. He was clearly out of his depth. "I'm not a dancer," he argued, desperately trying to make his point.

"I'm not a bubble-headed bimbo, but you want me to play Babycakes."

"That's different."

"Because Babycakes is a C. H. Battle creation?"

"Because everyone knows you're playing a part. They know it's not you."

Brigitte understood the distinction—even as irritated as she was. When he was being Fantasy Fuzz, he didn't have to be himself and expose the real Charlie Battle. To a man like Charlie—a very private man who shied away from people—that was a very significant consideration.

Would she ever really fully understand this man she'd fallen in love with? Could she accept his yen for privacy? She knew only that as she looked into his eyes, she saw both sincerity and vulnerability that warmed her heart.

"Does it have to be Family Night?" he asked.

Her face told him it did. Charlie realized they were at an impasse.

"If I came Wednesday, we'd have more time to think before I got there, and more time to talk."

"And you wouldn't have to risk being recognized," Brigitte countered. "You wouldn't have to take a chance on anyone finding out that Charlie Battle and Brigitte Dumont are an item."

"I don't care who knows! If I did, I wouldn't have asked you to come to New York with me."

"You don't care who knows that C. H. Battle and Brigitte Dumont are lovers. Charlie Battle is another matter."

Charlie looked so miserable that Brigitte hated pressing him. But she had to make him see what he was doing; to acknowledge the denial. She spoke softly. "You were quick to correct me in bed."

Charlie cocked his head, listening interestedly.

"That first time," she said. "When I said, 'Oh, Fantasy,' you were quick to tell me that it wasn't Fantasy Fuzz who'd made love to me, that it was Charlie Battle. Not C. H. Battle, the cartoonist, but Charlie Battle. All I'm asking is for Charlie to be as open with his affections as C. H."

*Oh, Charlie it probably seems like I'm asking for a lot, but none of it would hurt you. I'm asking you to grow, to stretch, to accept the part of you that's warm and loving and sociable—to be what you're capable of being.* They could make it work, she was sure of it.

She raised her hand to feel a lock of hair that hovered over his forehead. "You wouldn't have to dance. It's Claude's birthday and the girls are doing a special tribute. We wouldn't even have to introduce you, although I can't guarantee you wouldn't be recognized. You're a celebrity, whether you like it or not. And if someone happens to notice that we're a little chummy... Well, after our performances during the mystery weekend, you couldn't blame them for being suspicious."

Charlie moved his hands from her shoulders to cradle her face, and was struck by how soft her skin was against his weight-callused palms. Her fragility made her inner strength all the more impressive. She was strong in areas where he was weak. She wasn't afraid to walk in the world without disguises and pretenses, or to express her feelings openly and risk the vulnerability.

He knew in that instant that he loved her, would always love her. She would change his life; but his life was irrevocably changed already. It was now only a matter of letting her in, welcoming her, accepting the change—glorying in it. She deserved nothing less than to be celebrated.

"I'd never be ashamed to be associated with you," he said. "And that's from Charlie Battle's mouth."

He bent to give her something else from Charlie Battle's mouth—a kiss that was sweet, earnest, devastatingly sensual. "You've got a date tomorrow night, Babycakes," he promised.

Brigitte sensed the change in him—a capitulation, an acceptance. Hope suffused her—they hadn't finished their journey, but they were moving in the right direction. Gliding her hands up his chest and over his shoulders, she let her body mold to the length of his. "Let me give you something to think about in the meantime."

BRIGITTE FOUND IT difficult to concentrate the next day. Perversely, fate seemed determined to sabotage all her plans for Family Night. First Nicole came home from school in near panic, to announce that she'd forgotten about a choir rehearsal that absolutely could not be missed except under penalty of being expelled from the choir. Jennifer insisted she couldn't do the tribute to her father by herself, so they agreed to postpone the birthday celebration for a week, which left Brigitte with no program for Family Night.

Claire came up with the idea of doing an encore comic celebration of the Romantic Rites of Autumn that centered around the approaching elk-mating season, and offered to go through the Family Night files for the song they'd written for it several years earlier. That left Brigitte the task of finding Janet to make sure she was familiar enough with the melody they'd used to lead the kazoo chorus—only to discover that Janet and Stephen had seemingly dropped off the face of the earth.

The head cashier in Dumontique was vague, mentioning something about a doctor's appointment. Brigitte had to settle for leaving an urgent message for Janet to contact her as soon as she returned. By the time Janet called, Claire and Marguerite were nowhere to be found.

Brigitte's father offered the theory that they had gone into town to shop before dropping Nicole off at the school for choir practice. Jennifer had snagged her favorite cotton sweater and ripped a hole in it, and insisted that *no one*—at least no one twelve years old and cool—could possibly hope to survive for more than a few hours without a Mexx cotton sweater.

"Deserted in my hour of need!" Brigitte lamented dramatically, throwing up her arms in frustration.

"What's wrong, *ma petite?*" her father asked. His use of the pet name was reassuring.

"Family Night's falling apart, that's all. In two and a half hours the dining room will be filled with people, and we're going to look like a pack of dithering fools."

"Probably to no greater degree than on previous Monday nights," he teased. "If all else fails, we simply sing a few songs and you can dance with your *Père*. We'll do 'Tea for Two' tonight—it's been a while since we did that one, eh?"

Brigitte grinned. "Thanks, Père."

"Now, why don't you tell me why you're really in such a state."

"I have a date."

"With Mr. Battle?"

She nodded confirmation.

Jean-Pierre raised an eyebrow. "Perhaps I should borrow a shotgun, to make sure his intentions are honorable, eh?"

Brigitte giggled. "Oh, wouldn't that be a slice of irony."

Jean-Pierre gave her a wounded look, and she said, "You must have looked down more than a few barrels in your playboy days."

"There is a difference," Jean-Pierre pointed out. "Then, it was other men's daughters being trifled with."

Laughing, Brigitte replied, "Don't borrow that shotgun just yet. I'm hoping to inspire him to do the honorable thing without threat of force."

After leaving her father's office, she took care of anything that required immediate attention, then gratefully retired to a bathtub filled with scented water to study the notes for the opening ad-libs before dressing for dinner.

There was a knock at her door and she pulled her housecoat on without bothering to dry off first in her haste to answer it, thinking Charlie had arrived early. But it was Jennifer, who'd been dispatched to inform Brigitte that Janet and Marguerite were in the older Dumonts' suite practicing the music for the show.

"Thank goodness!" Brigitte said. "By the way, I like your new sweater."

"Thanks," Jennifer replied. "I got a turquoise one, too, and Nicole found a pair of ratty jeans."

"Ratty? Is that a new brand?"

Jennifer took amusement in her aunt's naiveté and giggled. "No. They're ratty—you know, ripped and raveled."

"And expensive, no doubt."

"She got some with rips over the knees."

"That sounds cold, with winter coming on."

"She wanted rips on the thighs, but Mama said no, because her butt showed."

"Good for your mother."

Jennifer shifted her weight from one foot to the other restlessly and eyed the silk dress Brigitte had laid out on the bed. "You're dressing up tonight?"

Brigitte nodded and smiled conspiratorily. "I've got a date."

"With Mr. Battle?"

The inquiry sounded a bit forced, and Brigitte eyed her niece speculatively, thinking she'd already known about the date and was playing dumb. "Uh-hmm," she answered.

"He's a hunk."

"Yes," Brigitte agreed. "He is."

He also proved to be late. So late, in fact, that they had to start without him. Brigitte lumbered distractedly through the opening ad-libs, finding it difficult to concentrate on a romance-minded, randy bull-elk when her mind was on Charlie and why he hadn't shown up.

She tried to be merciful, generous, open-minded, levelheaded, telling herself that Charlie wouldn't be jerk enough to stand her up without even a telephone call. The only alternative seemed to be that he'd met with disaster en route. She alternated between mental images of Charlie's body lying broken and bleeding along the side of the road, and Charlie's feet, cold to the point of freezing, beating a hasty retreat from commitment.

During the sing-along, she gave Claire a pointed look and eased away from the mike. She stole her way to the family table and slipped into the chair next to Stephen. "Any messages?"

Stephen shook his head sympathetically.

"He's either dead or hurt," she declared. *Or he's going to be, if I ever get my hands on him.*

"He probably had a flat."

"He's an hour and a half overdue."

Stephen shrugged. "Maybe he popped a fan belt and had to be towed."

Unconvinced, Brigitte returned to the stage. Everyone knew the show must go on, but Brigitte wondered what idiot had made that rule. Her thoughts remained focused on Charlie and the significance of his absence. It was lunacy for her to be standing on the stage, feigning enthusiastic interest in "The Ballad of Banff Barney, the Bull

Elk," when what she desperately needed to be doing was walking the floor, gnashing her teeth.

Finally they reached the last verse, and she was free to leave the mike to get her top hat and cane for the dance number with her father. At least dancing promised the opportunity to work off some of the restless energy of worry.

Claire made the stock introductory comments for the classic soft shoe. Brigitte waited with her father near the stage, outside the spotlights, while Claire and Janet led the kazoo chorus in one play-through of "Tea for Two."

"No word from Charlie?" she asked, knowing the answer before he shook his head.

Her father gave her a gentle smile. "He'll turn up, Brigitte, with a funny story about why he's late."

"Unless he chose not to come."

"Where is your faith, *ma petite?* Only a fool would make that choice. Your Mr. Battle does not strike me as a fool."

Brigitte danced by rote and found that the familiar steps of the routine she'd learned as a young child soothed her frayed nerves. As she performed her solo, she became aware of a ripple of distraction in the audience, but could see nothing but silhouettes beyond the spotlight that flooded her on stage.

Though she wondered what was going on, she was professional enough not to let it disrupt her performance. But when she turned with her arm extended, expecting her father to take her hand in his, a second spotlight popped on, illuminating not one man but two. On her father's face was a smile tainted with the bittersweetness of a man losing a daughter as he held her hand only long enough to guide it into Charlie's firm grip.

Charlie—in a sleek black tuxedo, white shirt and top hat! It was almost a contradiction, yet the warmth of his fingers and the love in his eyes as he smiled at her, mocking her surprise in his inimitable way, left no doubt that he was real. For the first time in twenty years, she missed a step, but quickly found her footing as Charlie fell into step with her.

*Kick left, kick right, kick left, kick right. Step, step, step, step, step—* Her mind teemed with questions as they danced, but foremost in her awareness was that Charlie was there—dapper, elegant, *and dancing with her*, out-Dumonting the outrageous Dumonts.

Her gaze met his as she shuffled past him, then swayed in time with the music as he shuffled past her. When? How? *Why?*

They ended with a flourish, as Charlie knelt on one knee and Brigitte perched on the other, still staring questioningly into his eyes.

"Romantic as an aardvark, eh?" Charlie teased, grinning devilishly at Brigitte.

Claire—where had she come from?—had stepped up behind them. "Ladies and gentlemen, the Chalet Dumont presents a romantic moment featuring our own Brigitte Dumont and Mr. C. H. Battle, creator of *Fantasy Fuzz*."

"Charlie Battle," Charlie corrected, as Claire thrust the microphone close enough to pick up his words. He was staring Brigitte straight in the eye. His demeanor changed then, to utmost seriousness. "Brigitte Dumont, I'm madly in love with you—will you marry me?"

What should have been a word came out as an emotional squeak as Brigitte flung her free arms around his neck and hugged him fiercely.

"That sounds like a yes to me," Claire said. The audience burst into applause, which intensified as Charlie, keeping her in his arms, rose to his feet and carried her from the crowded dining room.

Later, Brigitte would learn of Charlie's morning spent locating a tuxedo and his afternoon learning the soft-shoe routine from Stephen, and the fun Nicole had pretending to have choir practice so the birthday celebration would be canceled in favor of a tribute to romance. At the moment, she knew only that Charlie held her in his arms, that he loved her, that he'd asked her to marry him in front of a roomful of witnesses, and that he was taking her, with caveman instincts, to a place where they could be alone to start the rest of their lives together.

On the way out of the room they passed her two grinning nieces without noticing the thumbs-up signal the girls sent them or hearing the wistful sighs of two young girls—one in a cotton sweater and the other in ratty jeans—enchanted by romance.

## HARLEQUIN *Temptation*

### Rebels & Rogues

All men are not created equal. Some are rough around the edges. Tough-minded but tenderhearted. Incredibly sexy. The tempting fulfillment of every woman's fantasy.

When it's time to fight for what they believe in, to win that special woman, our Rebels and Rogues are heroes at heart.

---

Cameron: He came on a mission from light-years away... then a flesh-and-blood female changed everything.

**THE OUTSIDER** by *Barbara Delinsky*.
Temptation #385, March 1992.

Jake: He was a rebel with a cause... but a beautiful woman threatened it all.

**THE WOLF** by *Madeline Harper*.
Temptation #389, April 1992.

---

At Temptation, 1992 is the Year of Rebels and Rogues. Look for twelve exciting stories, one each month, about bold and courageous men.

Don't miss upcoming books by your favorite authors, including Candace Schuler, JoAnn Ross and Janice Kaiser.

**AVAILABLE WHEREVER HARLEQUIN BOOKS ARE SOLD.**

RR-3

# my VALENTINE 1992

Celebrate the most romantic day of the year with
MY VALENTINE 1992—a sexy new collection of four
romantic stories written by our famous Temptation
authors:

GINA WILKINS
KRISTINE ROLOFSON
JOANN ROSS
VICKI LEWIS THOMPSON

My Valentine 1992—an exquisite escape into a romantic
and sensuous world.

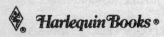

*Harlequin Books* ®

VAL-92-R

# Take 4 bestselling love stories FREE

## Plus get a FREE surprise gift!

## HARLEQUIN
## PROUDLY PRESENTS
## A DAZZLING NEW CONCEPT IN ROMANCE FICTION

### One small town—twelve terrific love stories

Welcome to Tyler, Wisconsin—a town full of people
you'll enjoy getting to know, memorable friends and
unforgettable lovers, and a long-buried secret that
lurks beneath its serene surface....

### JOIN US FOR A YEAR IN THE LIFE OF TYLER

Each book set in Tyler is a self-contained love story;
together, the twelve novels stitch the fabric of a
community.

### LOSE YOUR HEART TO TYLER!

The excitement begins in March 1992, with
WHIRLWIND, by Nancy Martin. When lively, brash
Liza Baron arrives home unexpectedly, she moves
into the old family lodge, where the silent and
mysterious Cliff Forrester has been living in seclusion
for years....

### WATCH FOR ALL TWELVE BOOKS
### OF THE TYLER SERIES
*Available wherever Harlequin books are sold*

TYLER-G